For Trena

Happy Birthday

February 1997

Fondly,

Helen

#5-
J12
F

D1011704

ALSO BY J. CALIFORNIA COOPER

Homemade Love
Some Soul to Keep
Family
The Matter Is Life

A Piece of Mine

J. CALIFORNIA COOPER

A Piece of Mine

ANCHOR BOOKS

DOUBLEDAY

New York   London   Toronto   Sydney   Auckland

AN ANCHOR BOOK

PUBLISHED BY DOUBLEDAY
a division of Bantam Doubleday Dell Publishing Group, Inc.
1540 Broadway, New York, New York 10036

ANCHOR BOOKS, DOUBLEDAY, and the portrayal of an anchor are
trademarks of Doubleday, a division of Bantam Doubleday Dell
Publishing Group, Inc.

A Piece of Mine was originally published in hardcover by Wild Trees
Press in 1984. The Anchor Books edition is published by arrangement
with the author.

Cover art: detail of a quilt, from *The Afro-American Tradition in
Decorative Arts*, by John Michael Vlach.
Copyright 1978 by The Cleveland Museum of Art.
Reproduced by permission.

Typeset and produced by Heyday Books, Berkeley, CA

Library of Congress Cataloging-in-Publication Data
Cooper, J. California.
A piece of mine / J. California Cooper. — 1st Anchor Books ed.
p.   cm.
Originally published: Navarro, Calif. : Wild Trees Press, 1984.
1. Afro-Americans—Fiction. I. Title.
PS3553.05874P54   1992
813'.54—dc20   91-27755   CIP
ISBN 0-385-42087-0
Copyright © 1984 by J. California Cooper
ALL RIGHTS RESERVED
PRINTED IN THE UNITED STATES OF AMERICA

DEDICATED
WITH LOVE TO:

Maxine Rosemary Lincoln Cooper, My mother.
One and only, PARIS A. WILLIAMS, My chile.
Joseph C. Cooper, My father.

My sisters and brother, Helen Shy Cooper,
Elvira Mitzi Walker and Joseph C. Cooper, Jr.

My Great and Grandmothers,
Marie Lincoln-Smith, Augusta Nero,
Addie Lovey Cooper.

My Great and Grand Aunts, Ellen, Clara,
Charlie Mae, Rebecca and Ruth.

Important others, Hazel, her daughter Patricia,
DeRethal and Opal,
Shirley Williams Ethridge, Mama.

All the female ancestors whose names I will
never know. I regret knowing nothing about
these important women in my life, whom I am
positive, struggled to survive, which is the
only reason I am here.

TO THE FUTURE

Kiska, Pamela, Lamont, Gigi, Teague,
Annette, Mia, Little Mimi, Landon, DeBoise,
Lavaundos, Joseph, Jr.,
And Me!

Acknowledgments

To Alice Walker and Robert Allen of Wild Trees Press, without whose encouragement and consideration my stories would still be sitting in a drawer, someday to be thrown out by someone saying, "These are useless." I will never be able to thank them enough.

To Howard Morehead, photographer, for giving me my first book on the written word years ago.

Margo Norman and Shy Scott for listening.

Paris Williams, for all the support a mother needed.

—J.C.C.

CONTENTS

A Piece of Mine

$100 and Nothing!

WHERE we live is not a big town like some and not a little town like some, but somewhere in the middle, like a big little town. Things don't happen here very much like other places, but on the other hand, I guess they do. Just ever once in awhile, you really pay tention to what is going on around you. I seen something here really was something! Let me tell you!

Was a woman, friend of mind born here and her mama birthed her and gave her to the orphan house and left town. Her mama had a sister, but the sister had her own and didn't have time for no more mouths, she said. So the orphan home, a white one, had to keep her. They named her "Mary." Mary. Mary live there, well, "worked" there bout fifteen years, then they let her do outside work too and Mary saved her money and bought an acre of land just outside town for $5.00 and took to plantin it and growing things and when they were ready, she bring them into town and sell em. She made right smart a money too, cause soon as she could, she bought a little house over there at the end of the main street, long time ago, so it was cheap, and put up a little

1

stall for her vegetables and added chickens and eggs and all fresh stuff, you know. Wasn't long fore she had a little store and added more things.

Now the mens took to hanging round her and things like that! She was a regular size woman, she had real short hair and little skinny bow legs, things like that, but she was real, real nice and a kind person . . . to everybody.

Anyway, pretty soon, one of them men with a mouth full of sugar and warm hands got to Mary. I always thought he had a mouth full of "gimme" and a hand full of "reach," but when I tried to tell her, she just said, with her sweet soft smile, "maybe you just don't know him, he alright." Anyway, they got married.

Now he worked at Mr. Charlie's bar as a go-for and a clean-up man. After they got married I thought he would be working with Mary, in the field and in the store, you know. But he said he wasn't no field man and that that store work was woman's work lessen he stand at the cash register. But you know the business wasn't that fast so wasn't nobody gonna be standing up in one spot all day doing nothing over that cigar box Mary used for a cash register.

Anyway, Mary must have loved him cause she liked to buy him things, things I knew that man never had; nice suits and shirts and shoes, socks and things like that. I was there once when she was so excited with a suit to give him and he just looked at it and flipped its edges and told her to "hang it up and I'll get to it when I can," said, "I wouldn'ta picked that one, but you can't help it if you got no eye for good things!" Can you magine!? That man hadn't had nothing!! I could see he was changing, done spit that sugar out!!

Well, Mary's business picked up more and more and everybody came to get her fresh foods. It was a clean little store and soon she had a cash register and counters and soda water and canned goods and oh, all kinds of stuff you see in the big stores. She fixed that house up, too, and doing alright!! But, she didn't smile so much anymore . . . always looking thoughtful and a little in pain inside her heart. I took to helping her round the store and I began to see why she had changed. HE had changed! Charles, her husband! He was like hell on wheels with a automatic transmission! She couldn't do nothing right! She was dumb! Called her store a hole in the wall! Called her house "junk!" Said wasn't none of that stuff "nothing."

But I notice with the prosperity he quit working for Mr. Charlie and got a car and rode around and walked around and played around! Just doing nothing! And when people go to telling Mary how smart she was and how good she doing and they glad she there, I heard him say at least a hundred times, "I could take $100 and nothing and have more than this in a year!!" Didn't like to see her happy and smiling! I think he was jealous, but he coulda been working right beside her! When he married her it was his business, too! I heard her tell him that and guess what he answered? "I don't need that hole in the wall with stuff sitting there drawing flies, I'll think of something of my own!" Lord, it's so many kinds of fools in the world you just can't keep up with them!!

I went home to lunch with Mary once and he got mad cause we woke him up as we was talking softly and eating. Lord, did he talk about Mary! Talked about her skinny legs and all under her clothes and her kinky hair. She tried to keep it up but she worked and sweat too hard, for him! She just dropped her head deeper down into her plate and I could see she had a hard time swallowing her food.

Then, she try to buy him something nice and he told her to give it to the Salvation Army cause he didn't want it and that he was going to give everything he had to the Salvation Army that she had picked cause it ain't what he liked! Ain't he something! Somebody trying to be good to you and you ain't got sense enough to understand kindness and love.

She cook good food for him, too, and he mess with it and throw it out saying he don't like her cooking, he feel like eating out! Now!

Just let me tell you! She want a baby. He say he don't want no nappy head, skinny, bow-leg baby and laughed at her.

She want to go out somewhere of a evening, he say he ain't going nowhere with the grocery bag woman!

I didn't mean to, but once I heard her ask him why he slept in the other bedroom stead of with her one night—she had three bedrooms—and he said he couldn't help it, sometime he rather sleep with a rock, a big boulder, than her. She came back in with tears in her eyes that day, but she never complain, not to me anyway and I was her best friend.

Anyway, Mary took to eatin to get fat on her legs and bout five or six months, she was fat! Bout 200 pounds but her legs was still small and skinny and bowed. He really went to talking bout her then, even in the store, front of other people. Called her the Hog! Said everybody else's Hog was a Cadillac but his was his wife! And laugh! He all the time laughing at her. They never laugh together, in front of me, anyway.

So, one day Mary say she going to take care some business for a few days and she went off alone. He say "Go head, do what she want to do." He don't care bout what she do! "Do whatever!" Just like that! Whatever! Whatever! Didn't finish it like other people do, like "Whatever you want to," just, "Whatever!" I guess he heard it somewhere and thought it was smart to say it like that. Well, when Mary come back, I coulda fell out cause she brought one of her cousins, who was a real looker; long hair, big busts, and big legs and a heart full of foolishness. Maybelline was her name and she worked in the store all day, I can't lie about that, she sure did help Mary, but where she got the strength, I don't know, cause she worked the men all night! In three or four months she had gone through all the legible men in town, some twice, and then all the married illegible ones, some of them

4

twice too. She was a go-getter, that Maybelline. But, she did help Mary and Mary seemed to need more help cause she was doing poorly in her health. She was sighing, tired and achy all the time now.

But she still took care of her business, the paper work and all, you know. Once, I saw Charles come into the store and she needed him to sign a few things, if you please, and he took them papers and bragged to the fellas in the store that "See, I got to sign things around here to keep things goin." He didn't even read them, just waved his hand and signed them and handed them to Mary without even looking at her, like she was a secretary or something, and went on out and drove off with a big grin looking 50¢ worth of importance, to me anyway.

Well, Mary just kep getting worse off. I told her to see a doctor and she said she had in the big city and she had something they couldn't cure but she wish I wouldn't tell nobody, so I didn't. But I felt so bad for her I loved her. I knew whatever was killing her was started by a heavy sad heart, shaking hands, a sore spirit, hot tears, deep, heavy sighs, hurtful swallows and oh, you know, all them kinda things.

Soon she had to stay home in bed. Wasn't no long sickness though, I could see she was going fast. Near the end, one day I saw her out in her back yard picking up rocks and I knew the dear soul must be losing her mind also and I took her back in the house and tried to get her to let loose the rocks and throw them away, but she wouldn't let go. She was sick but she was strong in her hands, from all that work, I guess, she just held on to them, so I said, "Shit, you ain't never had too much you wanted to hold on to so hold the rocks if that what you want!" And she did.

Now, she asked Charles to take Maybelline back to the city to get the rest of Maybelline's things to move down there and Charles didn't mind at all cause I had seen him looking that Maybelline upways, downways, and both sideways and I

5

could tell he liked what he saw and so could Maybelline cause she was always posing or prancing. Anyway, they went for a day, one night and back the next day. Before they went, I saw Charles sit on the side of Mary's bed and, first time I ever saw him do it, take her hand and hold it, then bend down and kiss her on the forehead. Musta been thinking bout what he was going to do to Maybelline while they was gone, but anyway, I'm glad he did do it. It brought tears to Mary's eyes. Then, they were gone and before they got back, Mary was gone.

I have to stop a minute cause everytime I think of that sweet woman . . . .

She had told me what to do, the funeral and all, so I had taken care of some of those things and Mary was already gone to the funeral home and the funeral was the next day.

When they come home or back, whatever!, all they had to do was get ready to go to the parlor. I don't know when or nothing like that, but when Charles went to the closet to get something to wear, the closet was bare, except for a note: "Dear Charles," it say, "They gone to the Salvation Army just like you always say you want. Yours truly, Mary."

Now that man run all over trying to find some way to get them back but they was nice things and somebody had done bought them or either kept them, you know what I mean? Then, he rush over to the bank to get some money and found out his name wasn't on the account no more! The manager gave him a letter say: "Dear Charles, You told me so many times you don't need me or nothing that is mine. Not going to force you to do nothing you don't want to do! Always, Mary."

His named was replaced with Maybelline's so naturally he went to see her at the store. She say sure, and give him $50 and he say, "Come go with me and help me pick it out," and she say she ain't got time. So he told her take time. She say, "I got to take care this business and close the store for the funeral." He say, "I'll close the store, this ain't your business to worry about." She say, "This my store." He say, "Are you crazy?" She say, "I ain't crazy. I'm the boss!" He say, "I'm Mary's husband, what's hers is mine!" She say, "That's true, but this store ain't hers, it's mine! I bought it from her!" He say, "With what? You can't afford to buy no store as nice as this!" She say, "Mary lent me the money; it's all legal; lawyer and everything!" He say, "How you gon' pay her back? You got to pay me, bitch!" She say, "No . . . no . . . when Mary died, all debt clear." He say, "I'll see about that!" She say, "Here, here the lawyer's name and number." He snatched it and left. He musta found out she was right and it was legal cause I never heard no more about it.

Now everybody bringing food and all, the house was full, but I was among the last to go and when Charles got ready to go to bed he say he wasn't going to sleep in the room Mary died in and he went into the third bedroom. I heard him holler and went in there and the covers was pulled back and the bed was full of rocks . . . and a note say: "Dear Charles, Tried to get what you wanted, couldn't carry no boulder, honest. Yours, Mary." Me, I just left.

Next morning he opens the food cupboard and it was almost empty, but for a note and note say: "Dear Charles, here is 30 days supply of food. Waste that too. Yours, Mary." I'm telling you, his life was going upside down. He and Maybelline stayed in that house alone together and that old Charles musta had something going on that was alright cause pretty soon they were married. I knew he thought he was marrying that store again, but let me tell you, Maybelline was pretty and fleshy but she couldn't count and didn't like to pay bills or the workers on that little piece of land of Mary's and pretty soon she was broke and the store was closed cause nothing wasn't in there but some old brown dead lettuce and turned up carrots and empty soda bottles and tired squashy tomatoes didn't nobody want. Charles didn't have nothing but an almost empty house. They cussed and fought and she finally left saying she wasn't really his wife cause she didn't have no divorce from her last husbands! So there!

Now, that ought to be all but let me finish telling you this cause I got to go now and see bout my own life.

Exactly a year passed from the day Mary had passed and a white lady and a black lady came to Mary's house with some papers and I heard a lot of hollering and shouting after a bit and Charles was putting them out. They waved those papers and said they would be back . . . and they did, a week later, with the Sheriff. Seems like Mary had give Charles one year to live there in the house and then it was to go, all legally, to be a orphan home for black children.

Welllll, when everything was over, I saw him sitting outside in his car, kinda raggedy now, just sitting there looking at the house. I took a deep breath and went to my dresser and got out the envelope Mary had give me to give him one year from her death, at this time. I looked at it awhile thinking bout all that had happened and feeling kind of sorry for Charles till I remembered we hoe our own rows and what we plants there, we picks. So I went on out and handed him the envelope through the car window. He rolled me red eyes and a dirty look and opened the envelope and saw a one hundred dollar bill and . . . a note. He read it with a sad, sad look on his face. "Dear Charles, here is $100. Take all the nothing you want and in a year you'll have everything. Yours truly, your dead wife, Mary." Well, he just sat there a minute, staring at the money and the note, then started his car up and slowly drove away without so much as "good-by." Going somewhere to spend that money I guess, or just stop and stare off into space . . . Whatever!

Sins Leave Scars

WHEN Lida Mae was born the ninth of nine children, she had a 90% possibility to do and be anything she would choose. She had a good brain and disposition, good health and body, excellent looks and big legs to come in the future! She was going to be neat, petite and all reet! As they say!

During the first 12 years as she was realizing her world of food, animals, insects, trees and flowers, school and other people, people, mostly men, were realizing her. Even brothers and uncles liked to put their hands and anything else they could where they shouldn't have been. She always had some change to spend and she was generous and kind to everyone and shared always. She liked to laugh. I mean, what did she know to cry about? So she was fun to be with.

Her mother, Sissy, was tired and worn out early from having fun because it seemed every time she had some fun, she had another baby! They were beautiful children though and each one a memory of some good time! The first one was her husband's and maybe one or two of the others. She didn't know and it didn't matter no-way! She had some money from the state and her own little odd jobs (not too many tho, she had been tired a long time now) so that in case, as usual, her husband didn't bring nothing home, she could feed them and him, too. Sissy was like that, treated everybody alike.

So Lida Mae hurried to school and to play, even to household chores with a smile on her pretty face. She lived by rote that way til she was 14 years old and was coming home from school and got a ride from one of her mother's friends, Smokey, who had a run-down raggedy car but acted like it was a new Oldsmobile or something. During the ride he drove real slow, the long way, cause he couldn't get enough of feasting his eyes on Lida Mae and all her innocent peachy splendor. She shone like a brilliant star in that dirty beat-up old pile of junk. She had accepted the ride cheerfully enough so he asked her to accept $1.00 first then changed it to $2.00 to let him touch her in her very own private spot. She seemed disappointed for a moment, but Lida Mae kept looking at the $2.00 on the seat til she said "I ain't gonna pull my panties down!" He said he could manage that and she opened her young legs and he managed it as she picked up her $2.00 and rolled it deep into her fist. She got out at home, at last, and he whispered "Don't tell your mama!" She answered "Are you a fool? I ain't gonna give her my $2.00!" and slammed the door and bounced on in her house!

Now, people don't have to be there to "know," you know? Somehow some people just looked at Lida Mae and knew something from their own experiences. Lida Mae had a few boyfriends her own age she laughed and talked and kissed with and sometimes at a show or playing hide and seek, they did just that: played hide and seek. She was not really a loose young girl or a prudish one, just caught up in the middle of life and didn't know a damn thing about it so she just "felt" her way through. Then, when she was 15 years old she was still a virgin because she also liked her school work, books and the teachers. She knew all about love leading to marriage and all that but she wanted something out of life because her teachers told her there was something to get out of life. She wasn't always thinking about boys.

But the unexpected is so unexpected it's expected! One day going home from school (she was really a doll at 15 going on 16) the man who owned the filling-station called to her and said "Hey, little bit! come over here and have a Coke with me! It's on the house!" Lida Mae, because of her fight for survival at the dinner table at home, seldom refused something to eat or drink for free. She smiled as she turned her feet toward the station, "O.K. Mr. Hammon!" He grinned down at her. "Let's sit inside, it's too hot out here!" "O.K." she smiled as she followed him. He opened the Cokes asking her if she wanted some whiskey in it and when she said "No thank you" gave her plain Coke. He sat down in the only chair pulling her by her dresstail down on his lap, "Sit down here girl, ain't got no other chair for you to sit on." Now, Lida had known him all her life it seemed so she wasn't nervous, she sat! He rubbed her leg through her dress while he talked to her, "Who your boyfriend girl?" he grinned. (He wasn't a bad looking man.)

"I don't know," she said smiling.

"You don't know who you love?" He looked shocked.

"I don't love none of em, I just like em!" She took a drink.

"I know they like you." He lowered his voice.

"How come?" She grinned.

"Girl, you know you pretty, pretty as a picture!" He rubbed her leg. "Even I could like you!" He was serious now.

"Oh, Mr. Hammon, you wouldn't! I'm too young for you and Mrs. Hammon wouldn't like that!" She took another drink.

"Mrs. Hammon don't know everything!" He smiled then noticed she was almost through with the Coke. "Wanna nother Coke?"

"No, I got to go now! I'll take one with me if you want to!" She set the empty bottle down and prepared to get off his lap.

11

Mr. Hammon moved his knees and Lida Mae almost fell backwards and Mr. Hammon grabbed her around the waist and under her dress as she struggled to get up. He said, "Oh! Oh! Lookit here what I got my hand on! I didn't mean to do it, but I couldn't let you fall!" He grinned.

"Well help me up!" She cried.

"I can't!" He grinned. "I can't move my hand!" But he was moving his hand and when he let Lida Mae up, she was mad! She left there with six Cokes tho and her virginity intact.

Lida Mae didn't play so hard with the boys for the next week or so. Something told her it wasn't so innocent and she felt a little grown up in a way they weren't.

Somehow on the next hot day after school when Lida Mae had no money, her long braids freely flying behind her, she turned into Mr. Hammon's filling-station. He was just a man after all and she felt grown so she went and got her own Coke and sat down in the chair herself! Mr. Hammon watched awhile as he worked on his customer, one of the few in this little small town, then she was leaving with six more Cokes, waving good-by. In a few days she stopped again and reached for a Coke but the Coke freezer was locked. Mr. Hammon walked over to her smiling as he unlocked it and held it open for her and told her to take two out. This day when she sat on his lap, she opened her legs and he smiled with the devil looking out of his eyes and she looked at him with eyes wide open to receive the devil.

It wasn't long before Lida Mae was not a virgin anymore and really liked Mr. Hammon. She had all the Coke she wanted to drink and kept a nice little piece of change in her pockets. She had new sweaters, blouses, skirts and shoes to wear. Things she had never had too much of except at Christmas, maybe. She didn't play with the boys her age anymore cause "she had a MAN," a grown man with money! She felt above her friends, girls and boys, until sometimes she forgot and played as hard as they did at games the way a young girl her age should have!

Mr. Hammon didn't care nothing bout no school; sometimes he told his wife he was going fishing instead of working and closed the garage and Lida Mae skipped school. He and Lida Mae stayed in back of the garage on the little cot Mr. Hammon had kept for such purposes for the last 20 years anyway. They drank Coke, only now they had whiskey in it and Lida Mae would get home drunk but nobody paid it no mind, there was so much else to pay attention to in a house full of nine grown and half grown kids: some of the older ones coming in drunk too. There were still some there that were 25 years-old or bout! Just lazy, do-nothings most of them. Some bringing a wife or husband home or go live off with one and be back and forth so you sometimes didn't know who was living at home and who was not! Sissy didn't get drunk so much anymore after the doctor warned her. Just laid around and never smiled, eating and sleeping and getting fat, but when she did get drunk they gave her plenty space cause she would tell them to get their grown asses out of her house! Then, she would grab her coat and stagger out the door to they didn't know where and they didn't care where! Just don't mess with their lives! I'm sure the devil used to look in on the situation and be amused!

Lida Mae liked herself because she had more sense than to settle for boys who could only make babies. Mr. Hammon wouldn't do that to her! He gave her money too! Now, how you like that!? She smiled to herself. SHE had a future! She was gonna stop cutting school too! The teachers had spoken to her and she was getting ready to graduate, but she had missed a few tests and things that she had to make up! So! This was the last day she was going to let him talk her into cutting class in the afternoon, she thought to herself as she turned into the filling-station.

She was telling him that as he was undressing her, he was already undressed when he let her in the back door. She was also taking a drink of her Coke and whiskey as he laid her down and was kissing her beautiful body all over, loving its

13

smoothness and softness. He excited her body and she put the drink down tho she wished he wouldn't hurry so! They were moving up an old road for him and a new and unfamiliar one for her.

BAM! The window next to the door was broken in and Mrs. Hammon looked through the opening! "Andy! Open this got-damn door!" She screamed, looking like a crazy woman in a frame. Mr. Hammon was speechless and could only stare at the broken window and shift his gaze to the door as she kicked it! He wished he could stop moving on top of Lida Mae, who was trying to push him off, but he couldn't. Lida was scared and wanted to run but he wouldn't stop and she began to have a climax just as Mrs. Hammon came through the window and lifted her knife and started trying to cut Lida Mae's face (which Lida hid with her arms) but cut her arms instead; then her husband was reaching for her, trying to stop her and hollering to Lida Mae to run! Get her things and run! Which Lida Mae, wide-eyed and frightened nearly to death and bleeding from numerous cuts, tried to do! She had to grab clothes, dodge the knife, open the door all at the same time. She was crying too and couldn't always see. Finally she got the door open and there were all those people who had heard the noise and come to see what was happening. Lida was naked and bleeding . . . what a sight! She had just begun to run when the knife flicked across her buttocks and she screamed as she ran into the arms of Smokey who "just happened" to be standing there with what looked like hate in his face. He grabbed her and helped fight Mrs. Hammon off because Mr. Hammon couldn't stay outside long with no clothes on, til he hit her on the chin, knocking her out, and put Lida Mae in his car to take her to the hospital.

They were almost there when he stopped the car near a wooded area. He slapped her already bloody face saying "Whatcha wanna go with that sucker for? I'm glad I told on you cause that'll keep your ass away from there!!!" She was in shock, so she couldn't say nothin as he wiped the blood away from her face and kissed her as he removed the clothes from her, laying her back. She started to struggle and he said "I just saved your life, bitch!" He slapped her again so hard her ear ring flew off through the window. He made sex with her, dirty as she was, and bloody, then drove her to the hospital and helped her go in. Needless to say she carried those scars the rest of her life, the ones outside . . .and the ones inside.

Lida Mae didn't get to her graduation. She did not want anyone to see her again, ever. The doctor had sewn her up; 72 stitches on her arms and buttocks. They had also decided to fix her insides (since she had already started trouble so young) so she would not be bothering the state with bills for children. She didn't know it, no one but the doctor and the nurse did.

When she went home, she was so unhappy there, her mother sent her to live with a sister of hers about 15 miles away in another little town. Lida Mae was glad to go. She packed her new long-sleeved blouses and the rest of her things and left without looking back.

She was very quiet the first month or two she lived in the new town. Going to church with her aunt who was very religious. School was out, so she helped around the house and with the few animals they had. Everything was fine and Aunty was pleased cause Lida was no trouble at all and she must be a good person cause the preacher started stopping by two or three times a week to visit and he never had before. He was watching his flock . . .he said.

Lida Mae knew why he was coming by cause he was always touching her when it was accompanied by words of the Lord. But, she wasn't having any of that! She thought about the graduation she had missed and her future that had stopped. She didn't want to be a domestic or a waitress so she had to think of going back to school or something! Well, "something" came up first, in the person of a friend of her uncle's. A nice older man about 55 years old, James Winston. His wife had passed on and he had a house, car, some land and some money and even tho he had another girl friend, Josie B., he was falling in love with Lida Mae. He wanted to marry her.

Lida Mae took about a week to think about it. She kept picturing the house and the car. She could have her OWN! Her aunt kept urging her by saying, "HOUSE, HOUSE, HOUSE." Her uncle kept saying, "Money, money, money." So Lida Mae took her young, inexperienced, naive self and married him and went home to her house!

Now, in the country, if you don't work or have something to do, the time stretches out long, long, long. You fill the days with eating, gossip or making love. Lida Mae's largest outlet was gossip! She didn't really know she was gossiping, she thought she was just telling a friend the truth about what she thought. But people can take your truth and stretch it, twist it, tear it apart, turn it inside out and when you get it back, you are making enemies and when you try to straighten it out, you talk a whole lot more and give the people new ammunition to shoot back at you and then you have made more enemies! So the days come to be filled with stinky shit and then you don't feel so good (unless it's natural to you) and you don't always know why. Then, you go to church and sing and shout and get a little off your chest and then feel better all day Sunday . . . for awhile.

It wasn't long before Lida Mae was going with the preacher. She just seemed to move naturally into situations without much forethought, but she really hadn't ever known anyone who gave her any idea of how or why this was done; only a few teachers in school regarding the future through education, and there was so much in her life that diluted those urgings to wise decisions.

Lida Mae was kind tho, she was good to her husband. The house was clean, his meals were cooked, his clothes were clean, but he drank quite a bit now and was usually sleeping it off nights. She was drinking more now and with some kind of confrontation at least three times a week on account of her mouth, she naturally turned to the preacher. It made her feel the affair was O.K. with God. It wasn't O.K. with God and it wasn't O.K. with Mrs. Preacher either cause one night she came over to see Lida Mae and when Lida Mae came to the door, Mrs. Preacher threw a pot full of lye water in Lida's face. It was a good thing her aunt was there; she cared for Lida's face and got her taken to the doctor. Lida's skin was young and healed well but her eyes were affected and they were cloudy and dim when she came from the hospital. I went by to see her and she said to me "Well, here I am, still young, done been cut up and now almost had my eyes burnt up! I can see, but not much. Not the things I want to see. Not the pretty world outside and not my pretty clothes. I don't want to go anywhere again. But, this is my house! I have given up a lot for it and done a lot to it and I don't want to leave it again ever, tho I do want to leave this town. I don't want no more of Mr. Preacher either! Oh he calls, and comes around! But I wouldn't open the door and if my husband let him in I went in my bedroom and shut the door til he was gone!"

But time passed and soon everything was back to "normal?" Lida Mae thought of school only briefly, just couldn't get the grit up to go. Thought of eye operations, but since she had to go out to some big city and she didn't want to do that either and her husband didn't want to spend all his money (course they wasn't his eyes) she didn't go. She seem to be seeing a little better every day anyway.

Time went by and this Josie B., who used to be Lida's husband's girl-friend, came to be friends with Lida Mae. I could have told Lida she didn't mean her no good cause Josie B. was still mad bout losing that house and money and a man. But Lida Mae seem to listen to you, then when she talked back to you seem like she ain't heard nothing you said! Anyway they became friends and they started going

17

out together to these juke joints that they have round here. Between that gossip and liquor and backbiting, Josie somehow got things fixed so one day when Lida Mae was high and sitting on a stool in one of those joints, Leella and Bertha jumped on her and beat Lida up! Even busting a bottle cross her mouth so that she lost four or five teeth right there in front. Well Lida Mae went right back in the house again and stayed there and in church for three or four months. She was about 20 years old now, but drinking so heavy (used to send her husband to the liquor store every day!) she looked like she was 50! Skin still smooth and all but them eyes and that mouth and them scars! Lord have mercy!

Then, one day, her husband stepped on a nail and only soaked his foot and in two weeks he was dead! Josie B. and Bertha came and sat outside the cemetery and laughed, drinking in their car with hatred in Josie B.'s eyes. I went to see Lida after the funeral, she was sitting on the screened in front porch still in her black dress with a record playing real loud saying "The sun gonna shine in my backdoor some day!" I talked to her awhile and she said one thing; she say "You know, I got this house, I got some money and a car . . . but I keep trying to see, in my mind, would I rather have my eyes, and my teeth . . . and my looks back and all these scars off . . . I believe I rather have nothing if I could just have myself back. OR SOME REAL LOVE! Ain't nothin left for me but love. I'm all gone."

She was young, but she was old! And through! But somewhere inside of me I didn't think she had to be.

Something good happens to everybody and about a year or so later a man came back to this town who had grown up here. He came to see his mama and saw Lida Mae at church (that's the only day she sobered up) and gave her his heart and stayed longer than he had planned. She took him in, used him, abused him . . . just tried to use that poor man up! She seemed to be mean, mean, mean! He was a neat, clean person with a little money, I guess, cause he was always running to the liquor store for Lida or bringing her candy, flowers and sweaters and things. Got her car fixed and all the work in her house that needed a man's touch. But she put him out every day when she through needing him for that day, cussing him. Now, she was playing that record bout the sunshine was coming in her back door some day and here the sunshine was coming in her front door and she didn't see it! Well, she was making him eat shit and nothing but a fool want to eat the same thing every day so he finally kissed his mama good-by and left, looking back, but leaving anyway! Lida Mae say "He'll be back! I put some of this good stuff on him! He be back!"

But he never came back.

The years have passed and we have really sure nuff got old. Lida Mae looks like she is 150 years old and she is only 45 or so. I stop over to see her on my way to my son's house to get my grandchild sometime and she still be setting on the porch, drinking and she say things I don't know if I believe them. She say, "Life ain't shit, you know that? It ain't never done a fuckin thing for me!!"

When I leave, thoughts be zooming round in my head and I think of those words I got on a 15¢ post card go like this:

Some people watch things happen.
Some people make things happen.
Some people don't even know nothing happened.

Then I go on over to pick up my grandbaby and thank God, ugly as I may be, I am who I am.

Who Are the Fools?

WITHIN these times there lived a man named Mr. Rembo and his wife, Teresa. Mr. Rembo was a 57-year-old, white-looking black man, square of torso, thick stumpy legs and wispy grey hair, rheumy light brown eyes and a stomach that overrode his belt. Mr. Rembo was the kind of man who, when he found himself alone with little girls, sat them on his lap, squeezed their thighs, tickled their titties, pinched their arms and slapped their little behinds. Consequently, he shelled out many nickles and dimes. Mr. Rembo also tore up his wife's Bible books and laughed at her as she would struggle to retrieve them. He would pull her down in bed on Sunday mornings, when she was going to church, to have sex, when he wasn't too hung over and sick from being drunk. Her only relief was when he went to his job as a night watchman.

Mrs. Rembo was a nervous, thin, 49-year-old, brownskin-ned, church-going woman always looking over her shoulder for an attacker, perhaps because Mr. Rembo often struck her for no good reason except he felt she was his to do with as he liked. Now, Mrs. Rembo wasn't really a fool, just kind.

She knew Mr. Rembo's mother had died after being kicked by a cow she was trying to milk during her ninth month and she gave birth to her son, Mr. Rembo. His father had married someone else rather soon, someone who did not like to take care of other people's children. Mrs. Rembo thought Mr. Rembo had been hurt enough.

The Rembos had lived in the same neighborhood twenty years or so and some neighbors didn't like him but couldn't put their finger on just why, just didn't! Mrs. Ginny, the next-door widow of two husbands did like Mr. Rembo, though, and spared no effort to show him, often asking him over for a drink or two of gin, while they laughed at Teresa's church-going ways and her fearful demeanor, talking about sex as Mrs. Ginny leaned over near him so he could slap her on her fat ass as she leaned back with laughter.

Mrs. Ginny didn't really like Mr. Rembo either; as a matter of fact, she just needed a regular sex life and since she didn't look too good, anymore, had to take what she could get and she didn't see any reason she couldn't get Mr. Rembo! When she needed him, that is! She had tried going to the church house for a while after that good-looking preacher had laid her mister to rest for the last time, but that talk about sin, adultery and hell and goodness and hell and heaven had drove her crazy with boredom and the preacher didn't pay any mind to her anyway . . .well, that was, in her words, "Enough of that shit!" In short, Mrs. Ginny was the type of woman to say, "Mercy Jesus! Got-dam! Amen!" as she orgasmed under someone else's husband.

Mr. Wellington, the grocer, had been the neighborhood grocer about four years before they moved into the neighborhood. His wife, Angie, had been sick for her last ten years and had been dead already for two years. He had loved and taken care of her till the last day. He missed her. He saw, in Teresa Rembo, the same sweetness and gentleness his Angie had had. He had, also, seen her change from a neat, good-looking woman into a thin, nerve-wrecked, deep furrow-browed, old, unhappy woman. Once when the store was empty he had pulled her to him and pressed himself to her and held her out of his own desperation, for he was a faithful husband. She had not moved away, only looked sad as though thinking of something long, long ago, and gone. He had kissed her and though she had kissed him back, she had not come into the store for a long time. He had never done it again, but they seemed to have a delicate bond of some sort.

He had also spoken to her since his wife died saying, "Teresa, we are getting old, you are too old to keep being treated like a fool! If you want to leave that man and get a divorce, I'll marry you and take care of you. If you don't want me, you can still work here while you get yourself together, I'll help you." She had looked at him and shaken her head at the futility of it all. He reached for her hand and said, "We both need someone to give our love to." She leaned toward him as if to say something, decided against it, took her packages with a sad smile, and left. He could not know he had made her heart soar like a broken-winged bird dreams of, because it was months before he even knew she had been really listening to him and that came about like this.

Teresa used to go into the bathroom to read her Bible and study her books, locking the door. Mr. Rembo had been drinking steadily all day at Mrs. Ginny's and at home. He was sloppy drunk and decided to have some sport. Kicking in the bathroom door, one of the few things still working in the house, he tore into her, cursing, "I knew you was in here reading that shit! Don't you know there ain't no God yet? Got-dammit! If there was, what he gone want a dried-up ole woman like you for, ain't good for nothin?! But there ain't! There ain't no God!" He began to tear up her new Bible. "See? If there a God, why don't he snatch this book outta my hands? Ain't this s'pose to be his holy word?!" With book leaves going every which way Teresa screamed, "Stop, stop,

stop!" and struck him a frail blow on his fleshy shoulder. He came up from bending to reach for another book with a backhand slap that threw her into the tub where she hit her head against the faucet and began to bleed and cry (she had never cried before).

Mr. Rembo raged, "So you gonna shout at me?" He was enjoying himself. "Yeah, you gonna hit me, too! You losing your mind?!" He pulled her roughly from the tub and shoved her through the doorway into the kitchen. "You dumb bitch! I said God, not you! Why don't he help you? Cause he ain't there, that's why! I don't want no more Bibles in my house! You hear? You hear?" He pushed her out the back door roughly and she sprawled on the ground. Now, this was to the delight of Mrs. Ginny, who was looking through her window, though, I must add, with a fleeting pang of sympathy for Teresa.

Mr. Rembo went back into the house and returned with the scraps of her Bible as Teresa was on her knees trying to get up. He threw the scraps over her and, placing his foot on her behind, shoved. This time when she hit the dirt, she didn't try to get up, just sobbed, long deep, sad, tired sobs.

Mr. Rembo slammed the door shut, saying drunkenly, "You betta realize I'm your god! Stay out there till you ready to ack like it!!"

Now Teresa laid there so long that Mrs. Ginny would have thought she was dead if she hadn't seen the movements of a sob every once in a while. "Oh get up from there and have some pride bout yourself!" she said to the gin bottle.

After a while Teresa did get up, slowly, brushed herself off and walked away, with dignity, though bruised, dirty, torn, with rivulets of tears making rows in the dust on her face. She walked to Mr. Wellington, who closed his store and took her to a lawyer without using a comb or a washcloth or anything else on her first. Then, he took her to a doctor . . .then he took her home . . . his home.

Mr. Rembo slept about an hour, then weaved his way to

23

the back door and seeing she wasn't there, weaved his way through the house calling her name. Deciding she would be there eventually, he weaved his way over to Mrs. Ginny's to get another drink. At her front door, which she opened a crack, she said quickly and in a low voice, "Come in the back door, come in the back!" To her humiliation, he peed right by the geraniums, then staggered to the back door. She wanted not to answer the door but somehow had to, and did. They spent the evening and many other evenings drinking because Teresa never did come home. However, things changed. There was not so much laughter. He was morose and often drunk when he came, whether morning or night. He knew where Teresa was and wanted to go get her but since she had been to the divorce court, they had warned him, so he didn't, but told everybody she was living in "sin" with Mr. Wellington.

His attempts at sex with Mrs. Ginny seemed pathetic and heavy. He drunk, she half-drunk. Mrs. Ginny seemed to be reaching for so much, trying to get all of something and he seemed to have nothing to come get. They only continued doing it because they both had a need to be close to sex, however unfulfilling it might be. He needed to show Mrs. Ginny, also, what Teresa was missing, and couldn't, so he just kept drinking.

Mr. Rembo's days became darker . . . he lost his job after being found drunk there. They tried not to fire him but after a dozen times or so, had no alternative; after all, he was supposed to be a "watchman!" He began to bald but the remaining hair seemed always tangled. His eyes seemed more rheumy and were often matted with the mucus that crawls in the eyes at night. His hands shook as he reached for the bottles of warm beer he liked. His mind was in a thick soupy fog. He hadn't been over to Mrs. Ginny's in several days. He didn't like to think of that last night.

Mrs. Ginny had held his soft penis in her hand as she stared at the ceiling, listening to his drunken snoring. Tears had seemed to want to come to her eyes but couldn't find a place to break through. She had fallen asleep without letting him go. He had awakened later, and lying still to remember where he was, he looked at the faded wallpaper, pieces hanging here and there, a cobweb from the ceiling to the window, a home discarded by some spider. The sheets seemed tired and old and wrinkled and felt damp around him. He felt her hand and removed it, finger by finger until her hand dropped away. Turning his head to the side, staring at the wall, two deep dry sobs shook his body trying to get out of his mouth, which he would not open.

Morning came and another bottle. Though it had been a year, his rage returned, stronger. He took his knife and cut all Teresa's clothes and threw them in the yard (which Mrs. Ginny came out and picked through, but because of her size found only a shoulder shawl and a purse that hadn't been cut).

Everybody knew Mrs. Rembo was now Mrs. Wellington. Mrs. Ginny still shopped there but Mr. Rembo never went near. Today, though, as he drank his gin and warm beer it was all he could think about. She was still Mrs. Rembo to him! She belonged to him! To him! Not to Mr. Wellington, not God, not nobody but him! He shouted to the house "Me! Me! She is my wife! Mine! I can beat her if I want to! She's mine! I can kill her if I want to!" The words hung in the air around his head, echoing, from the top of his sodden brain to his sick liver and sour stomach then back to his sodden brain. He cried. Tears and snot mingled as he rubbed his face with his hands. He felt no comfort, only rage. He put his knife in his pocket, and slightly staggering, went out the front door, to the corner and turned right for the two blocks to the Wellington store.

When he reached the store, he passed looking in from the side. To himself, he had become wise, smart, and slick. He stopped just past the store and tipped back to peer in from the corner of the window. Mr. Wellington was behind the meat counter waiting on a customer. Teresa was not in the store, but he knew the door to the right, just inside the store, led into the main house. When two ladies with children went in, he pressed close behind them and veered off to the right behind the counter and gradually made his way to the door and went through as Mr. Wellington bent down to take something out of the cold storage counter.

When Mr. Rembo stepped into the nice, clean, fresh-smelling, quiet house, these things stopped him. He felt suspended in time . . . but in a little more time his aura oozed into the air and he was able to penetrate the goodness of the home. He took out his knife and stealthily made his way through, reaching the bedroom where Teresa, after a morning of good loving, was sleeping with a slight, gentle smile on her face. He proceeded toward her but when he reached her he did not recognize the plump, smooth-skinned, smooth-browed woman with the softly curled hair with one arm thrown out in abandon. He was confused. A relative? A friend? He backed out of the room, turned and stumbled through the door toward the store. The noise awakened Teresa and she said, "Baby?" full of softness and love and warmth. The sound hit his ears, ricocheted, passing his eyes to his stomach up to his chest and down to his buttocks, first one then the other, then back to his head as he burst into the store.

Mrs. Ginny had seen him leave his house. She knew by instinct he was going to the store. This she was not going to miss! She reached for the nearest thing, the shoulder shawl, and followed him. When he burst into the store, her back was to him and he turned directly to the shawl and raising his knife, brought it down into her back. Again and again. Mr. Wellington had a large soup bone, a cow's leg, in his hand and he flew to stop Mr. Rembo and struck him with it. WHAM! Each time he struck, Mr. Rembo struck with his knife. SLASH! WHAM! SLASH! WHAM! SLASH!, till he fell to the floor beside Mrs. Ginny amidst the screams of the terrified customers.

The trial didn't take long and he was sentenced to death. Between each electric shock that was killing him, he screamed, "Oh God, help me! Oh God, oh God."

Loved to Death

DEAR Mr. Notebook: her heart, soul and body was filled with love and she was well hated for it; she loved liquor, men, song and dance and laughing. She loved God too but she didn't have time for Him. She loved her two daughters but she gave them away, but only to people who she knew loved them too. She loved learning but she couldn't do any reading cause everybody loved her wouldn't let books stay in her hands! I did all the reading cause nobody loved me enough to bother me! Late nights or early mornings musta caught her coming or going! She was like a lone thread, waving in the breeze longing to be part of a woven fabric of life, but the weaver couldn't catch her, she didn't have time! I'm talking bout my sister, Zalina. But, Mr. Notebook, you know that cause she's in all your pages running through my life and yours.

Ahhhh, I hurt all over . . . AHHHHhhhhhOhhhhhhhh, all outside and all inside! I wished she was dead so many times when we were young cause she was so pretty and I was so ugly! Uncomely, the Bible says! I wished it, but I didn't mean it! I didn't like her then, but I loved her! I know she loved me.

She was the second child born to my mama, but she wasn't my daddy's! Now everybody understand if the first child might not be his, but if the first one is and the second one ain't, that's a bad sign in a husband and wife!

Zalina knew it and always said she was a "love child!" I wanted to be a love child too, but what kind of love could I represent with this spine all crooked and legs going to the side, face looking like somebody threw my nose and mouth, eyes and ears at me and they hit and stuck all wrong? My daddy is half Indian and I got his long straight hair; Zalina got short kinky hair, but when that natural stuff came out and that hair was all picked nice around her face and that smile . . . she was just beautiful sunshine! When she smiled, the sunshine just spilled out all over you! You could have long straight hair all the way to the corner and back but wouldn't look no better than Zalina and her short hair!

Zalina wouldn't stop bothering mama bout being a love child so she told us Zalina's daddy had made her right in the bedroom next to where my daddy was sleeping a drunk off! She said he had been kind and good to us, helped us keep going sometimes . . . a good man and she kinda loved him. That's what made Zalina a love child I thought. But I also thought he might a been a good-hearted man but he wasn't no good-minded man making a baby in another man's house like that! A real good man would only make love and his own babies in his own house!

We all grown now, but I told my mama I wish I had been a love child like Zalina but just look at me! She said, "A love child ain't in the looks itself, it's in the life itself!" I wished I had told her earlier, I could have packed that in my heart years ago and used it when I needed it; it would have kept my heart from being so empty, just rattling round in my crooked chest!

You know how people forget you when you sit quiet and still for a long time? One night, I heard my daddy say to mama: "Xevera ain't mine, is she? Zalina is my child ain't she?" And mama say: "Your child is who you love. They both my children!" I didn't like to look at him for a long time after that! My own daddy! Not only was I not a love child, I wasn't nothing without my mama! And Zalina, of course.

When we was growing up, everybody always tell me "Sit down and rest!" But Zalina always say, "Come on! Run! Run!" I was scared to . . . just wanted to stand and cry. But one day, she pulled me and I HAD to! And I did! I felt the whole world turning under my feet! I just laughed and cried and Zalina just threw her head back and laughed so happy with me! We went "ring around the rosy" out there in that field with the trees waving at us. Lordy! I was playing! Ever after that I ran when I was alone or with her. It makes the world look happy to me. I still do it and I'm a grown woman now raising Zalina's and my daughter. I don't know who the father is and I don't give a damn!

I remember Zalina always look so ripe even before she hit her teens . . . like a ripe juicy plum or peach or like a watermelon so plump and sound so good when you slap it! Peoples were always slapping her behind, even daddy! Mama used to make her call all the salesmen and bill collectors "uncle" and tell her to run to em and hug em round the neck and kiss their cheeks cause we didn't have no money to pay em. Daddy drank a lot sometimes, you know, and didn't always go to work and when he did go and got paid, sometime we wouldn't see him nor the money! Well, Zalina would do what mama say and the men would slap her behind like she a little child but she wasn't no little chile anymore. Even me, sitting in my chair watching everything could see their hands linger or slap too many times. Afterwards, Zalina would go in our room and lay cross the bed and cry sometime. I'd go in there and say, "What you crying for? He left the radio here!" Or something he had done left. She would answer me, her face all mashed in the pillow with no case on it . . . "I don't know."

"Well, if you don't know, don't cry."

She say, "Just something I feel, but I don't know how to splain it." She had a nice soft voice. I hated to see her cry.

I say, "Cause of hugging that bill collector?"

She say, softly, "yea" and give one of them deep sighs like old Mz Wright do when somebody break in her house when she gone to church and take her only money.

I say, "Well, why do you do it then? Let him take that ole radio!" (I loved that radio too; it was all I had to talk to sometime.)

She say, "Cause I don't think mama like me to do it either, so I must hafta . . . if we both don't like it and still she tell me to."

I don't say no more . . . just think . . . sit and think. I am a good thinker. Then pretty soon mama bring us something, a piece of candy or half a orange or something and Zalina smile and forget.

At least I think she forgot.

Then, I remember so clear, one night, daddy came home and came in our room. I thought it was by mistake then, but now I know it wasn't, and he tried to get in bed with Zalina but she fought him. We was older then, bout 16 or 15 or something. I kept grabbing daddy telling him that was Zalina not mama! Then, I thought he might be playing so I jumped on his back and was gonna play too, but mama came in in the dark, didn't put no light on just stood there and he got up and left. Zalina just lay there crying softly into that pillow again. (That pillow sure could tell some stories if it could talk!) I remember wondering why a person so pretty and had everything, looks and all could always be crying? I kinda knew, but didn't know exactly what I was knowing. Anyway, next day when Zalina try to talk to mama, mama say, "Don't tell me . . . NOTHING!"

Zalina cry, "Why mama? He hurt me!"

Mama say, "Cause he all I got! Ain't got no more! Can't get no more! Got no money but his and (pointing at me) I got that chile there to take care of . . . the rest of her crippled life! That's why!"

31

Zalina start crying, "Why don't you love me, too? Don't I need somebody to love me too?" Mama slapped her even as she said, "I love you! But I got to keep a HOME! You hear me? A home! A home!"

Zalina say, "We can take care of ourselves! Keep our own home!" She mad too!

Mama say, like she had a 500 pound sack of rocks on her back, "Chile, you be gone from here in six months, a year, next month even, when the right man cross your path and you want to follow! Me and your crippled sister gonna have to stay here ... and live!" (I'm getting tired of that "crippled" word. I seem to grow a foot smaller every time she point at me. The house seemed so black and scary inside even tho it was early morning and the sun was out!)

Zalina went and threw herself on the bed in our room and cried in that pillow again. I always follow her and say something. I said, "Don't cry Zalina, he didn't mean to hurt you!" She looked at me a long time, not mean, kinda with love in her eyes, soft-like.

"Yes, he did."

I say, "Well, don't cry, he won't do it again! I'll kill him!" Lord, I was talking bout my own daddy, but I was talkin to my own sister!

She say, "I know it!"

I say, "How you know it?" (relieved).

She say, "Cause I'm leavin here!" And when she was through restin, she just walked out that house and didn't come back for a long, long time. So ... Mama was right ... I guess.

Then, I went to getting and keeping a heavy something in my chest thinking bout what my mama said when she pointed to me. I was the one making both of them miserable! Taking things and doing things they didn't want to. So I went (took me all day, I have to go slow you know) and looked up a job keeping babies. They had to be little new babies, cause I can't keep up with big bad ones. I found a job and after a few years of keeping babies day and night, I found a little house on a little clearing I could buy with my little savings. I wasn't scared way out there like mama said I should be, cause nobody hadn't never wanted me before, no way. The ladies still brought their children for me to keep by day and sometimes night, so I made a little money every week and kept taking care of myself. Then, didn't nobody really have to take nothing on account of me, no more!

But you know what? Mama still didn't leave daddy and you sure couldn't say things was any better with them!

Mr. Notebook, you remember when Zalina come back cause I wrote in on your pages. I was so happy to see my sister! I ran to her! She came in a big shiny car with a big shiny man. Lord! They all three was beautiful! Dressed to the "T"! She still had that sunshine smile and used it all the time, especially when she looked at that man! Him too! He smiled all the time and laughed a deep good strong laugh. He was always crushing her to him, too. Like they say in the books, "He crushed her to his heart." I told you she looked like a fresh plump fruit! Like if you squeeze it all the juice come splirting up! Nobody ever crushed me cept once a girl I had to fight til Zalina run out the school and showed that girl how not to bother me no more! First night she spent with me, she made her husband sleep on a cot in the kitchen and she slept with me and we talked and laughed nearly all night and I wondered why I had ever wished she would die.

Anyway, she brought us all, me and mama, some pretty things from the city and one of em was a pair of high heel shoes for me! I say, "Girl, what am I going to do with these? . . . I can't wear these things!"

She say, "You a woman ain't you?"

I say, "But I'm a cripple!" (that word again).

She say, "A crooked spine don't make a cripple. A crooked mind do! You wear them shoes even if you only wear them at home by yourself! Love yourself! Enjoy yourself! No matter if no one else ever do!" I just stared at her and loved her.

Pretty soon, too soon, they was leaving. Mama wanted to go with her, but Zalina say "You got to stay here and take care of your home, mama. I got to go and take care of mine!" So mama stayed home. We all three be taking care of each of ourselves. Zalina gave me her address case I ever need anything, then they were gone.

Wasn't long after that when daddy died from drinking so much, the doctor say. I got a ride to town and sent Zalina a telegram saying "Daddy is dead." She sent one back say "O.K." and that was all.

The next time Zalina came home, she brought a baby girl with her named Glory. She still looked good but something was missing beside her husband. Some of her smile. I soon found out (you know, I ask questions), her husband was killed because he was protecting his wife and his manhood when his white boss tried to rape Zalina. She said later on she pleaded with the white man and even let him do it to her so she could save her husband. But the white boss did it to her and still had her husband killed. Oh Lord, why she have to be so pretty that white man had to want her? Wasn't the wife he had enough?

She had a smaller car and all, but she still had pretty clothes, only this time she was drinking kinda heavy. She stayed with me mostly, but mama some, and mama kept the baby. Mama sure did love that baby and daddy was gone so she gave her whole self to that baby, little Glory.

Zalina found some friends in town so they could bring her some liquor. That was O.K., but I was disgusted when she took up with Murky Mac! An old dusty nothing man who didn't work but always laid around street corners and all. They would go into the bedroom and when they come out, he would always leave her two or three bottles of liquor. I ask her why she go on with Murky Mac like that? That even me, a virgin who really want to see what loving is all about and didn't never have no dream I ever would, would not let him come near me and put nothing of his in me!

She say "I don't like Murky Mac! He is a dirty old man! But he got the money to bring me what I want! And, I don't let him put nothing in me either! He just like to lick it and since he know how to lick it and I need something done to it, I let him!"

Well now!! Licking it! Don't that beat all?! Anyway, she finally got tired of us and left going back to the city. Said she would write me, and she did, when she got an address.

After she was gone, Murky Mac came out to my house and leaned on the doorjamb looking at me. I happen to be putting on my high heel shoes, for myself, you see, because I am a woman! I stared right back at him and pretty soon we talked. It was burning hot outside and I knew he didn't want to get right back outside in that heat, so I said "Might as well sit down and have one of your drinks!"

He said, "Might as well," and did.

Then he say, "You might as well have one too!"

I said, "Yea, might as well," and I did!

We had some more after that and Murky Mac said, "You might as well do it all!"

I say, "All what?"

He say, "Don't bullshit me!"

I say, "O.K., I won't bullshit you!" and I didn't.

He say, "Come on then."

He took me into my own bedroom and lay me down and . . . I did. It was alright too. My first time at anything, but nothing but that licking cause I still had pride about myself! And he was Murky Mac! When he left, he said "I'll be back!"

Well, I got a ride into town soon as I could and bought some little bottles of perfume cause I didn't see how he could stand it! Next time he came by, I put that perfume everywhere on me I thought I needed it! It musta worked pretty good too, cause he kept coming back after that, even bringing me presents, pretty little things . . . for women . . . for a lady . . . for me. I started thinking of something new to do. Tied ribbons on the hair, braided it sometimes, put jam on it, homemade. He liked lemon pie so I put some of that on it one time and when he left he took the pie off with him too. Well, I was having quite a time then. You know it, Mr. Notebook, cause I sure told it to you!!

Now about that time, a year or two later, Zalina came home again. This time, she came on the bus and brought another baby. It was another beautiful girl child, another beginning for me from Zalina.

Well, Murky Mac came out with the liquor for her, but only went into the bedroom with me! ME! Over Zalina! Some of her teeth were brown and her hair was just pulled back with a rubber band. Her clothes weren't too good this time . . . maybe that's why . . . But I don't like to think so! I like to think it was cause he loved me . . . or somethin.

She was drinking twice as much and looking twice as bad. Zalina left town again, but it didn't really matter because soon Murky Mac was dead and with him my ~~sex~~ love life was dead. Just dead. But I had a baby—Zalina's baby—and my life really began again. The baby, Mae B., was sickly a little bit, but I nursed her right on up and today she is a beautiful child, my child, our child, mine and Zalina's. I don't give a damn who the daddy is! And Mama don't care who the daddy of Glory is! That child has given her new life now she has the money from the state and her jobs to take care of a child right! They're both beautiful wholesome girls!

Oh, my sister, my Zalina, how I hurt for you.

A few years later, Zalina came back. She was sick. I could see it right off! She said the doctor had told her if she drank one more glass of liquor it could kill her! She said she hadn't had a drink in a whole week and she wanted to rest. How she would lay and stare at her children! Have you ever seen love in somebody's eyes? I mean just pouring out so you can SEE it?! Well, I have . . . out of Zalina's.

Time passes and Zalina got better and got to looking really good! Lots of people have moved to this town and

Zalina met up with a nice man who came to take her out. He even stop seeing his regular girl. Zalina really liked him and wasn't too long before they were talking bout getting married. Everybody always loved Zalina. But you know how people can be jealous and ugly and don't like you cause of their small hurts and minds and memories? Somebody told him about all kinds of things, true and untrue I guess, even about Murky Mac and maybe some things I didn't even know yet or either, and they made that man change. Zalina waited outside his job and his house so she could sit down with him and straighten things out, but she shouldn't have done that cause then I could see he really loved himself! She didn't suit him no more and he wouldn't tell her why, just married up with his first girl. Zalina went off and got three bottles of liquor and sat down and started drinking, talking bout being "tired." She would drink and sleep and wake up drinking again. That last bottle sent her to the hospital and that's where she died three days ago . . . and today, they buried all that sunshine six feet under the ground . . . and it hurts me. I hurt all over . . . inside and outside. AHHH-hhhhhh-ohhhhhhhhh!

Lord, Mr. Notebook . . . I don't know. I guess this may be my last time writing in you now that Zalina is gone. She put all the life in me, she put all the life in you. I ain't got no life of my own worth talking about. Just ain't got no life of my own.

I think about changing this name Zalina gave our baby from Mae B. to Zalina Two. No . . . no. I'm gonna leave her name to Mae B. Maybe some day . . . Mae B. just may be somebody on this earth and not just on your pages, Mr. Notebook. Cause, you know what, I'm going to teach her about how people can want you . . . can love you to death! Just use you up!

But right now . . . I'm going outside and run with Mae B. and think of Zalina while this earth that holds her spins round under my feet.

Say What You Willomay!

I'M telling you, say what you willomay, these mornings, early like this, is just too beautiful! People think that here in the country there ain't nothing but boredom, day after day. But they wrong! These is big days following great big days! Lookit them trees down that road and that big fat cow over there! And that sun coming up! Now, ain't that pretty?!

And I'll tell you something else! See that speck way down the road there? That's Laylonny. Coming to wait for the bus to get to work, just like us. You new here so you don't know her yet, but I remembers when she was born. Was a song out then bout Hawaii; Sweet Leilani! And Laylonny's mama loved that song so she named her baby "Laylonny." She couldn't spell it the way they did so she spelled it "L—A—Y—L—O—N—N—Y." Now Leilani may mean "Heavenly Flowers," but Laylonny must mean earthly flower! See what I mean?

Anyway, Laylonny was a fine girl, grew up good, good to her mama and all and got married up with the Jackson boy when they was both young and thought they was in love. Say what you willomay, we all goes through it! But they love didn't catch on and hold cause that boy took to beatin up on her! Yes, he did! Now the first three, four times he did that she just took it with a smile cause she didn't know nothing yet, but after while, when she hafta be lookin at all them marks and bruises and a black eye or two for a week or more, she commence to understanding that that wasn't no love to cleave to, so that girl packed her good sense up and left him!

Well, honey, say what you willomay, some mens don't know what life is all about. After she left, he commence to try to get her to let him kiss on some of them same spots, including her behind, but seem he had done beat and kicked em too much already for that so they never did get on no more! No! She moved back to her mama's, who had done got down sick, and commence to taking care herself and her mama! Oh, I tell you, say what you willomay, she is a good woman!

But you know what, it's some strange things in this world. That girl's mama didn't like her no more! Don't know was it because when that chile was young and she was raisin her, she had been a little wild, you know? And might not have liked to think her life was over and all the good times gone. Cause her daughter was so good lookin! And built so good! And still had some good times to look to. I don't know, who knows bout people anyway? Do you?

Well, anyway, the county was givin that girl some money to care for her mother and buy food and she was doing just that. But one day that damn fool woman told the visiting social lady that that girl didn't do nothing round there and didn't need no money. Well, they cut that stuff right off! The money! And that woman, Laylonny, had to get out of there and get a job AND go rushing home to take care of her mother, BOTH! And did it! Well, pretty soon it was pretty clear that Laylonny's mother was going to die . . . and everybody commence to going over there doing what they could and mongst them was one or two fellows who could see how good Laylonny was and how good she was to look at, and the one who had done lived in the city awhile, saw a big difference between her and them city women. Say what you willomay, there IS a difference! Now, he took up a lot of time with her and soon her heart was gone again and just after her mother passed, they got married up!

Now . . . I know they was happy and she still was a good woman cooking, cleaning, working part time, all that, you see what I mean? But he could not stand her dipping snuff and she dipped snuff, you know. And spittin in her little cup alla time. He would DIE if they had some company or he had a man friend over and she had a lip full of that snuff! Lord a mercy!! He did not like that!! He threatened, he raved, I don't know what all he didn't do to break that woman's habit. Tried to get her to smoke them cigarettes even, but she didn't like that. Everything! He tried everything! And do you know, say what you willomay, there be some fools out here! That man let that snuff run him away from his happy home! Well, I guess it wasn't so happy then, like it had been. But, instead of saying, "go wash your mouth out so we can kiss awhile," he just up and left, back to the city. Left his job and everything!

Wellll, no sooner he got back to the city, he got hold of a ciety lady, like he wanted, I guess, and you know, she didn't dip no snuff. And didn't do nothing else either!! Chile, that woman (my son told me this, he go to the city sometime) liked $100 suits and dresses, diamonds and furriers! She didn't do NO cookin! You hear me? NONE! Not even breakfast before a man go to work! He had to take her out every night he didn't order something brought in! Heard she wasn't too clean, either. Say what you willomay, some people look so good and clean when they come out, like they fresh out the fruit stand, but when they go home it's like that fruit thrown in a garbage can!

Anyway, he wasn't REAL dumb and so he soon got to seeing which way the arrow pointed and jumped into that

car of his which didn't have no fender on one side in the
back and a dent on the other fender (all that had happened
since he been back in the city). Anyway, he drove right on
back down here thout quitting his job up there. Went
straight to his old job and got that back, then went to my
son's house and cleaned up and slept some and I know for
myself, he went and circled Laylonny's house SEVERAL
times fore daybreak!

Now, that next day . . . it was a beautiful day, just like this
one, only a little rain drizzling while the sun was shining,
devil whipping his wife, you know? And she was coming up
the road like she is now, and that man was in that car just a
following side her real slow like she walk. She prob'ly went
slower that morning so she could get to hear it all, you know
how we womens are. Well, he was just a talking to her trying
to splain what all everything was and she would nod her
head and look off into the trees. Every once in awhile she
would say something, I don't know what cause I can't read
lips yet! By time she got to the bus stop, he done jumped out
that car and runned and grabbed Laylonny. Now I don't
know was it rain or tears running down Laylonny's face, but
it was all twisted up like crying do you. And when that Ralph
man grabbed her and squeezed her she just simpered and
sputtered and that juice in her lip shot out, just here and
there, not a lot, you know, and maybe a little trickle down
her chin and all. She musta spit when he was getting out the
car. Anyway, she really broke into crying then! When she
seen that snuff getting out, here and there, and he was justa
trying to hug her and kiss her and turning her head, she say,
"No, no, I got snuff in my mouth, Ralph!" And he grab her
head with his hands and held it still and said, "I love you! I
don't give a got-damn if you do!!!"

And I'll be hot-damn if he didn't mean it! That was four
years ago and they still together!!

Good morning, Laylonny!

41

Funeral Plans

I SHOULDN'T be tellin this secret, but you can just call me Ms. Can'thelpit cause I just can't help it! I got to tell it!

You can say what you willomay but I believe the Lord gives you something every time something else is taken away! If you got half a piece of sense, you will find that to be true. Just call me Ms. Senseless cause it has taken me so many years to truly know what that means and then I learned it from someone else . . . one of my friends, Willetta. I call her "Letta."

Letta and me kinda grew up together in this little one horse town, but I believe no matter how small a town is, it's still got some of every kind of people the whole world got in it.

Letta's people was as good to her as two poor people could be. She was their only child, and the Lord had sure blessed them in that one thing. They both worked hard. The mama sewing and cooking for white folks and the daddy farming his own little piece of land and doing odd jobs and also working at the plant just outside of town there. They must have loved each other too, another blessing of the Lord's,

42

cause they sure needed it. Letta studied hard in school cause they was planning for her to go on to college and she really was smart! Me, myself, I just dreamed of getting married someday. Ms. Dreamy, you could call me.

But when Letta was just past fifteen years, her mama had taken a nice lunch over to her daddy's job at the plant, and as the devil would have it, one of them evil white men who was sitting in his tractor, having only a warm beer for his lunch, decided to "play" a game on Letta's daddy and slowly backed that tractor up and claimed, when he planned to stop, the tractor kept goin backward! Well, Letta's mama and papa was crushed up bad! The mother lost her legs, had to have em both cut off! And her daddy's ankles and knees and hips, and shoulders was pushed together and he never could straighten out again. Leastways the doctor didn't think there was no big reason for goin through too much trouble for em cause what was they good for anyway? I heard that myself cause I use to, and still do, kitchen work for some of the best folks here in town, and I hears a lot! You can call me Ms. Goodear, cause I got em! Well, say what you willomay, you got to know what's goin on around you, if for nothin else cept to stay out the way of other folks' tractors!

Well, back to Letta and her troubles! The plant said it wasn't no fault of theirs cause it was all in "fun," not at working, so they didn't have to pay nothin! Nothin! The hospital sent a big bill, and I don't know what for, cause Letta's mama and daddy came out of that hospital just like they went in, bent up and crushed! Ain't no pills in the world worth all the money was on that bill! Letta just put that bill in a drawer and shut it! Was a nice white man and his wife her mama had worked for came over and had the house fixed to Letta's name and the hospital couldn't take that when it tried, so the bill just stayed in that drawer . . . for 25 or 30 years till she threw it out, til her mama and papa died, cause that's how long she taken care of them!

And I mean she took care of them! That's why I said they

was blessed! Neither one could move! You had to put them to the pot, put them to bed, get them up, set them up somewhere and feed em, all of it! She did it! I use to feel so sorry for them two people . . . just set and face and stare at each other all day long and sometimes tears comin down one face for a while and then the other, til Letta make them smile bout somethin. She kept them clean and the house clean. I would hear her sigh, them great big tired breaths sometimes but she didn't never act mad cause her life had changed so. Future all gone. Present gonna stay forever, look like.

Oh, people came over at first, preachers and neighbors, to try to run her little house and business but she didn't want none of that, said she wasn't no child. She was proving that! Sho was! I helped her all I could.

Now, Letta had helped her mama work, cookin, sewing, and washing, so she just kept doin these things and she took to doin hair in her kitchen for a few friends and so she was able to make it. She sold some of their things what was valuable to them, watches, clothes they was never goin to use again, the piano, things like that. But not her mama's wedding ring. She used to get so mad and frustrated and she would cry! Chile, there wouldn't be nothin to eat! But she never sold that ring, it stayed right on her mother's finger! Said, "my mama got to have something!" Well, they did have something! Her!!

I don't have to tell nobody who ever worked for money for a livin, how hard it can get to keep goin on. Letta suffered plenty hardships and went without almost everything! Some days, she didn't eat, but mama and daddy did! Many a night she didn't sleep, just tossed, cried at first, but finally just tossed and thought . . . hard. No candles or electric lights at night . . . save that money! Don't burn that little bit of firewood, go to bed and cover up. She could sew, but couldn't sew for herself, so her clothes got pretty full of thin places and she was still growing. Some of her old friends, the stupid ones, laughed at her when they see her in them clothes, glad to see her not lookin so cute anymore. She would get so disgusted, but I never did see her get mean and bitter. She just try to keep carryin on . . . and she did. Things got better over the years tho. Now I say that and the sayin goes so quick! To say "a year" takes less than a second I bet, and for Letta, a year, each year, took 365, 24-hour days. Long years.

Letta's sewing got mighty fine and the best people used her, and I mean USED her. They paid her half of what it should have cost, but they knew she needed whatever she could get, so that's what they paid her, whatever they could get away with. And her bakin stuff she was turnin out was truly beautiful to see and sho nuff good to taste! She had taken them tools her mama-dear had given her and turned them into blessings and a full way! She was a full provider long before she was 20 years old.

I had done got married bout that time and had two little sweet children I was raisin. They so sweet when they little! Me and my husband bought a little land and we builded a little house with our own hands. I loved my home and, come to think of it, Letta even came over there once to give us a hand on our house! She was somethin! Call me Ms. Admirer cause I sure admired her!

Some mens did too, but when they come over to her house and see those two skeleton-like bodies sittin there all day and her fixin for them and them just staring and sometimes droolin, well you can't catch everything right away, you know? Well, they just lost heart or never had it in the first place, I guess. Mens! They want to "fool" around, say that's what she need to relax her body! But she didn't want none of that! She say she did WANT it but not that way, cause one more mouth to feed by herself, and she would kill everything in that house! Letta had to be more tired than even I thought cause Letta had a good heart, not mean at all and wouldn't just ordinary think of killin! Anyway, they never got married to her, so she was alone . . . that kinda alone . . . man and woman kind.

Well bout 25 years or so after the "accident," Letta's mama died quiet in her sleep and Letta didn't say it was a relief or not. Just hugged and rocked her mama til they took her away, then she put her mama's wedding ring on a chain and put it round her neck. I said, "Why don't you wear it on your finger?" I didn't add the rest of what I was thinkin bout she wasn't never going to get one of her own, but that's what I thought . . . she was bout 40 then, or more! She told me, "No! I want my own weddin ring on my finger!" Well, you can call me Ms. Hushmouth, cause I sure know when to do that!

My husband had been dead five years or so, then. Worked hisself to death, in the cold and damp, days and nights of our life. Making food, finding food, going for medicine at nights in the rain, walking babies when he needed his sleep and I was sick and couldn't, so many things. He was a good man . . . my good man and my world. But one night my world slipped away from me and I was alone to raise my children. Course, I had my mama's help, but I got to know a little more what Letta was going through, had gone through all her life. You could call me Ms. Tired and Sad, cause that's all I remember bein . . . tired and sad.

Letta's father lived on another four or five years then he passed away too. She buried him lovingly, too. I began to look at Letta kinda funny then. Was somethin wrong with her? I mean, how can one person do everything right? Was she human? This was goin too far! She was too good to be true! I got kinda mad at her . . . not jealous . . . mad! She was my friend, but I didn't like her bein so good! Well, you can just call me Ms. Shamed cause I'm shamed I forgot all she had done been through ALL her life. The Lord had to have given her strength and there I was getting mad at her for havin it! Just call me Ms. Shamed! How I know how tight she was holding on? Or how close she was to lettin go, losin her hold? Well, I done already told you once, you could call me Ms. Senseless!

Two or three months after the father passed, Letta came by my mama's house. I had done lost mine, my husband built for me. Had taken a few loans out to help my kids in some personal and sickness problems and taken a few more later on for some police problems and the kids had done moved away somewhere else and I couldn't pay them notes and so they took my million dollar home for $400, and I moved back to my mama's. She was down and I was taken care of her anyway. I loved her and she had been good to me. She was dyin too tho. Well, she was old. Hell, I was old! Seemed like I was always just between life and death, life and death. Scared of life and scared of death. Call me Ms. Scared, cause that's the way I was runnin then.

Anyway, Letta stopped by the house one day and said, "I want you to bring me some of them fancy ladies clothes magazines from your job sometimes, if you will, Ms. Friend." She always call me "Ms. Friend."

I said, "I sho will, Letta. You mean the real fancy ones?"

"Real, real fancy, Ms. Friend."

"You want some of the recipes magazines?"

"Yea" she smiled, "bring some of them too, I got a plan!"

"You got a plan?" My ears perked up.

"Yes." Her smile was what you would call BRIL-LI-ANT. "Been thinkin about my life . . . now that it's mine to do with whatever I want! All mine!" I looked at her and she did look rested and better and I would say younger except you don't have to be younger to look good! So I asked her, "You ain't gone fly off to no big city and leave me here is you?" I laughed, but I sho didn't want her to go. Misery lovin company I guess, but . . . well, shame, shame, shame. She laughed back, "No, I'm too tired for a big city. I just want a good husband and I got a plan to get the kind of man I want . . . I think!"

"Plenty of these men roun here want to marry you now,

Letta!" She frowned up her face "Yea, now that I ain't got any problems! But they the ones with the problem now . . . they are all poor, cept for the ones already married, and I have decided I do not want a poor man or a poor nothin! I have already done all the poor I can take! Sides, I want to be in love and be loved!" I was gettin excited cause I wanted to talk bout things like this and never did know I had anybody to talk bout them with! I said, "I would just like a man of my own!" She answered me right back, "I don't just want a husband, a man, Ms. Friend, they ain't all that hard to get. I want somethin special! Somethin different! Somethin else from all what I know!"

I couldn't say nothin but "YEA!"

She went on, "See, I got this plan. Now I may not win at it, maybe I'll lose at it . . . but one thing, I won't regret tryin it! I want LOVE and I think I know somethin!" She laughed a little girl laugh, "Anyway, I got a plan!" She left then and I wanted to follow her home and talk some more but I heard my mama callin me. I thought about her plan and love all night. I rushed to work so fast the next day the lady I work for musta thought I was goin crazy and if she hadn't given me them books, I might've gone crazy for real all over her.

I took them magazines over to Letta's soon as I could cause I wanted to hear bout that plan! She was playin her new second-hand piano when I got there. She was takin lessons again for the last year or so and was soundin real good! She was playin a spiritual, with great big dips and curves and deep bass bumps in it! You can just call me Ms. Spiritual, cause I loves them! The house was beginning to look different. Not new but with more life in it. New curtains, slip covers and things like that. Say what you willomay, hope shows! Anyway, we got together over them books and this is what Letta told me. She say, "See, I been close to death for years and years. It don't scare me none. I've even seen some beauty in it. Death is mighty powerful but it can be kind and gentle too. And I done been to a lot of funerals, too

48

many maybe, but I plan to go to a lot more fore its over."

Now, I lowered my voice to the correct funeral tone and said, "Oh, I hope not Letta."

But she said, "Oh I hope so! Not wishin nobody to die, still they gone do it whether I want them to or not! And I been noticing . . . if a woman die, a man is left alone! If a man die, his friends come to the final hours and some of them is single and good men!" Well, right there I began to see. You can call me Ms. Quicksee now! She went on, "Well, I can sew and now I got a little extra money to spend on myself, I been makin me some beautiful clothes, bettern any I ever seen anyone wear round here!"

Well, she sure was right about that! That sewin can sure help your closet!

She went on, "Only chance I get to dress is for a funeral! And I'm the best dressed thing there! And everybody brings food and my cakes are the best lookin and best tasting, except for the real old ladies been bakin a long time, cause I been makin them for a livin! Now, I'm readin these French recipes and Italian recipes and I'm learnin plenty new ways to make a cake look like a angel baked it!"

Well, she was talking to her friend so a little braggin didn't hurt nothin!

On she went. "I'm playin the piano better and better, so now is my time to stretch out! There is funerals around here up to 20 or 30 miles away I can go to, and even further out where I have some relatives! Why, Ms. Friend, I can find a good husband if I just make the best funerals!!"

Well, she looked so happy and hopeful I didn't have the heart to say how terrible it all sounded to me. She saw my look tho and said, "You better quit frowning and try to get your own self together! You too young to be alone the rest of your life less you want to be! Do you want to grow old all by yourself?"

I shook my head "No" cause what she said was true, I was too young! I also didn't want to keep runnin behind some bush with a man what wasn't mine, every now and then only, you know?

"Well," she said, "this can work for you too! Start doing somethin with yourself! Do you feel old?"

"No!" I shook my head again.

"Well, you bettter get on the ball and bounce up and do some planning of your own!"

"Yes!" I nodded, my head like to flew off, and you can call me Ms. Grinning cause it suddenly seemed alright! I grinned my butt off all the way home cause I had a plan too! That's the first day I really cleaned that house up and cooked a full, delicious meal for me and mama in a long time, since my husband died almost, cept for holidays!

Letta was ahead of me tho, she was still slim from all that work she used to have to do and she could really do her hair. And she really read them books and could copy a pattern down to the ace degree! Me, I decided I would settle for a medium kind of man. Well, facts about it, I had to! I had let some things go down I never would get up no more!

Letta started going to them funerals and taking cakes to the wakes and things. She would play the piano AFTER the funeral. She said, "No jobs, just sit and cross them clean pretty legs and look around."

Sometimes Letta went 30 miles or so . . . on the bus! She had to win! She had what it took! Bout four months later, a very well to do mortician asked her to play chamber music sometimes before the funeral. Like, you see, come early. He was single and bout her age. His business was bout 35 miles away and he took to sending a car for her. A big, long black Cadillac. She was in style! Chile! Other mens came to see her but she wouldn't carry on with none of them. She said, "I might like somethin they do and end up in love with a poor man and I don't want to, so if I am not around them, I can't grow to like them!" That was that!

She always came home on the same day she left at first, but pretty soon, she didn't come home the same day! Her and

that mortician was getting pretty close. Then one day, she
stayed home three weeks without going anywhere. Told me,
"I like that man and I could love him, but I don't want no
job. I want love and a husband and that's what I know I can
get! Hope it's him, but if he ain't right, he can do it with them
dead folks for all I care! I sure could love him though!"

I was so busy going to funerals and learnin how to sew I
didn't see her for a little while, a week or two, but when I did
see her she flashed a smile and a engagement ring on me
and you couldn't tell which one was the brightest! She began
to drive her own big car, I don't know what it was, but it was
not black! Well, Letta married that mortician and it's like her
life just started! I been over there to see them, at the funerals, you know! They both look like they in love. He watch
her with such pride, she watch him like to say "I'm glad I'm
where you are." Funeral long gone out of their minds and
they right there in the middle of it! "I understand" she tells
all the bereaved.

Me, I'm still working the plan, for real now, sho nuff!
Cause the other day at a funeral, a man got up to say
something bout the deceased. I'm learning all the words
now, I used to say, dead or passed on. Anyway, he happened
to say he wasn't married. He just bout my size too. I liked his
looks. After the funeral, when he was blowin his nose and
wiping his eyes, I walked over, patted him on the back and
said, "I understand." He looked at me real bright and
reached out to shake my hand and hug me. I paid good
attention to how it felt to be in his arms, had to do it real
quick but I liked it. I invited him home to a good ole-fashion,
home-cooked meal. I didn't take time to be smart like Letta.
When he accepted and we was on our way to my house I
wondered if he had a plan too! But I don't care. I'll tell you
somethin, they say a good man is hard to find, well, a good
woman is too! Anything good is hard to find and if you got
any sense you don't want nobody else's. Like me, I want
mine! So, when we was walkin along and talkin you could

just call me Ms. Happy Hopeful cause I was!

So, now I am cuttin him a piece of dessert cake I just made this morning from a new recipe. See, I got a lot to share and you can catch more bees with honey than you can with butter, so now I'm goin on in my fresh clean livin room where this new man friend of mine is helpin my mama get comfortable and take him some of this delicious cake! You can just call me Ms. Honeybunch, cause I'm on my way!

He Was a Man!
(But He Did Himself Wrong)

I HAVE always been the kind of person who wonders about people and things and I have some neighbors who have kept me pretty busy with plenty to wonder about! It's not real important how or where Smitty and Della met, the main thing is they were married nine years when I got to know them. At first, because of the way the world looks at things, they seemed an unlikely, funny couple. He was short, 5 feet or so, 125 pounds, while Della was 5'7" or so, and 207 pounds. You pictured them making love and in your mind it was real funny, but you shouldn't do that picturing stuff because making love, real love, is never funny! Remember the heart has its own way of picking a partner and never asks for measurements.

Anyway, Smitty was a feisty, loudmouthed, bragging, aggressive little man. Always trying to out-talk or out-do some taller man. But Della loved him even beyond the love-is-blind thing. Anything Smitty did was alright with Della.

I mean even the way she cooked his meals; he had so many things he disliked and his food had to be just right. I mean JUST RIGHT! He was the kind of man who even liked gravy on his lamb chops! Very few vegetables, hardly any fruit and all that! All of which made Della gain more weight because of course she had to taste it to be sure it was just right. She could make home-made bread that would make you kill yourself. She did everything, Della did. Wash, cook, clean, garden, shop, chauffeur, watch football games, listen to him lie, pet, massage and make love too. Maybe more, you know, I don't know everything.

I know he was proud of Della, he was always bragging down there at the pool hall and at work about her, but he never told her, thinking just staying with her was enough. Well, after nine years, maybe he was right. Their marriage musta been strong because they got over some real big hurdles which made me wonder at the way it all turned out.

Like, one time I ran over to their house. They had a nice little house, sitting all by itself on a neat little lot, that they rented. Anyway, I went over there and he was standing on a box directing her how to tie a rope over a beam so he could hang her. SHOUTING "I am the man! You gon have to do what I say! I ain't taking NO shit!" Della just crying, trying to tie that rope like he telling her. Well, I talked them out of it that time. I think he was glad because he didn't know no other way to back down and give her her life back. I told her later "You are a fool! Big as you is, you gonna let that littler man kill you? Help him kill you?!" That's when I found out it wasn't the first time. Anyway she just said, "I don't think he was really gonna do it!" and smiling, went on about cooking him something special. I just really want you to know she thought he was special, that he had power, black and otherwise! Whatever he said she believed him. I mean . . . that man had him a woman!

Now there's always a little hell waiting round paradise and Della's hell was that every once in awhile, Smitty hit her, abused her. It hurt and it didn't hurt! But it seemed to do so much for him, being so small and all, hitting a woman so large, she never tried to hit him back. He would tell everyone down at the pool hall and work (again) that "I know I am boss!" He pranced as he told them, his chest stuck out in pride, he had a lot of that! He had whipped his woman, all 207 pounds of her! . . . all those pounds that loved him.

Their bed had to be braced up by bricks underneath so the mattress wouldn't tilt when Della got in bed and bring him crashing over to her side, reminding him of his size. One night when they were sleeping, someone broke into the house. Don't know what they came for cause Della and Smitty didn't have nothing much special. Just one of these crazy people that don't have sense enough to be honest and ain't got sense enough to know how to be dishonest and rob somebody with something! Anyway, Della heard the noise and woke Smitty up. He lay there a moment then said, "Let's go see what's going on." He hollered from the bed, "Who's there! Who's in this house?"

They got up and went into the hall and there was this dope addict or something looking raggedy and holding a gun. Smitty ran past him, going to get his gun, I guess, and Della got scared and tried to follow him past the robber, who was then squashed against the wall with Della screaming at him to let her go! She must have hit him or something, he was really trying to get out of that tight spot with all that mouth wide open screaming in his ears, and probably hoping somebody would come in and save him from his victims, but their house stood all alone and the cafe-bar across the street made so much noise, nobody could hear them. The gun went off around that time and Della thought Smitty had saved her when Smitty came rushing around a corner hollering Della's name, guess he thought she had been shot, and the robber slid down the wall at her feet, dead.

Smitty hadn't been able to find his gun. They grabbed each other and looked at the dead man; he had shot himself with Smitty's gun . . . accidentally. Della said, "We gotta call the police!" Smitty said back, "Wait a minute! Let's talk about this!" So they did. Smitty continued "Now listen . . . if we call them cops we gon have a lot of trouble! That's my gun! And I ain't got no license for it! And I can't prove I didn't pull that trigger and put that gun in his hand! All them cops look at TV and ain't no tellin what they gon decide happened here!" Della's eyes grew even wider. "Well, what else can we do? We can't throw him outside in the street!" Smitty shot back, "Oh yes we can! That's just what we got to do!"

He ran to look out the window with Della following him, her large white flannel gown billowing around her. No one was in sight and the music blasting from the cafe. It was settled in Smitty's mind . . . the dead man was going outside. Della started crying til Smitty slapped her into just whimpering and sniffling. She went to get her robe and a cap and Smitty went to get an old blanket out of his car. She noticed the blood that had flowed from the man's wound and went to get a bandaid, Smitty came back and snatched it and stuck it in the man's shirt pocket. In fact, they did all the wrong things you see on TV. They rolled the man up and when the cafe closed and all was dark they carried the corpse over to the empty lot and left it! Went home, cleaned up, wiped off the gun, put it back in the drawer and went to bed with Smitty explaining, "I didn't kill him, you didn't kill him, so we ain't got nothing to do with it! He broke in our house, took our gun (everything was suddenly "our") and shot his own self! We didn't know him before, we don't know him now! So go to sleep and forget the whole thing!" . . . So they did. See, what I mean, something that's big like death, they stepped over that like it was a broom!

Anyway, the police found the body the next day, took it somewhere and did something and since the man was black the case was closed, even with all those clues, stamped "killed by person or persons unknown . . . CLOSED!" and that was that. Smitty and Della picked up their life and went on as usual. He felt real smart cause he had handled it real smart so he began to add, when they had arguments, "You ain't got no sense! If it wasn't for me, a man in this house, ain't no telling what would happen to you!" Della smiled at all that, she was used to it and she loved her Smitty!

Then this thing happened that made me wonder at them because they had been through such big things and this seemed little to me, you might say.

It was a day that Della had not been feeling well; maybe lost a baby or something almost as important; she was always talking bout having a baby and Smitty was always trying to make one. Also, her special cake for Smitty had burned while she was trying to untangle something in the washing machine wringer and when she put the cake on the sink, she burnt her hand and in flinging her arm out she hit the filled dish drainer rack. It fell to the floor and dishes and glass flew everywhere! She was barefoot and cut her foot tipping across the floor. She burst into loud, dreadful tears and ran into the hall past the sign that read, "God Bless This Home" through the pink door she had painted because pink made her feel like a woman going into a romantic bedroom. She flung herself across the bed onto the spread she had crocheted painstakingly to laugh and love on. She cried herself to sleep.

When Smitty came home, he did his lion's roar at the door and receiving no answer he went through the house and found Della asleep and . . . he got mad! He started stomping around and shouting at her about the dirt (there was no dirt). The filthy kitchen (just broken dishes, that's all). No dinner (well, there was none, but my lord!) The messed up favorite cake (as if it was on purpose) and anything else his little mind could come up with! He never did ask her what was wrong. He kept shouting, "A man this and a man that."

Della swung her legs around and sat on the edge of the bed and tried to smile and explain. She was still trying to smile and explain when Smitty came rushing up and slapped her twice! One way and then back the other! Her arm must have shot out instinctively in reaction and she caught him solid and he flew all way cross the room, through the door and hit the wall in the hall and blacked out! Now, that alone was bad enough but Della went and picked him up and placed him in bed! That Della was strong! So when he woke up, an hour or so later, he looked around him and . . . cried. Now he really was a man, ain't no question, but he cried . . . him! . . . Smitty!

Della came rushing into the room at the sound of the crying and when she saw him she started crying too. "What's wrong? Are you hurt daddy? What's the matter, baby?" But he pushed her away, snot and spit flying, then he snarled at her from his pain . . . an ego can be a dangerous, painful thing. "Get away from me! Get away! I hate you, you big, fat, ugly bear! You a ape! A gorilla! You ain't no woman!"

"But, Smitty," she began to whine and try to ease him but he wouldn't have any of that! He got up trying to move without showing his pain and got the little raggedy suitcase (they didn't never go anywhere so they didn't need no new ones) and began to throw things in it. Della's eyes were big and red and swollen, she kept trying to grab his shirts and underwear from him, but he done stopped crying now and was really talking mean to her, calling her all kinds of names, sloppy fat bitches and things like that! It was untrue and it hurt her. You could almost see her drawing up, shrinking, every time a word struck her. Seemed like the words were razor blades cutting her to ribbons. This was her Smitty talking to her!

As Smitty got to the door he turned, "I can't never live with you no more! You always gonna think you bettern me! That's what you want . . . to be the man! Well, I ain't staying nowhere I can't be the man! You get yourself and your stuff together and get out of my house as soon as you get you some money! I'm takin all we got now cause I done made it all while you sat chere on your ass! You the man now, you can get you some more!" Della reached for him, "Please daddy, baby, please daddy, don't go! Don't leave me! I'm

SORRY (she screamed that). I didn't mean to hit you! Please don't go! I'm begging you! Daddy, I'm begging you!" She grabbed his arm and such a hate in his face went down to his arm and he struck her so hard she just let go and stood there with her arms hanging, and her tears pouring, down. He left, leaving the door open so she could watch him leaving, wobbling away dragging that suitcase, taking the car. She finally shut the door and went to bed, for two weeks.

I tended her and checked on her but she wouldn't eat nothing or talk and usually she's a big talker. But time takes care of everything and time took care of her. Pretty soon she got up and got on out to find work. She was still grieving, but with every bad there's some good and she was losing weight like thunder. Smitty had got him a room somewhere and was busy telling everybody everywhere that he done left Della, "Wasn't gonna keep no woman who wants to be the man in his family, Della didn't know how to treat no man but she would before he sat foot in that house again." He meant it too . . . he said! But every day when he come out of that door at work, lunch and quitting time, he seem to be looking for somebody. Pretty soon, he would go to the windows and peer out all through the day, but nobody was there . . . least not Della. He let everybody know where he lived, but she didn't go there either!

I caught her one day, just a cussing to herself, crying. I said, "What's the matter with you Della?" "Nothing," she answered, "Just repeating all the names Smitty called me so I don't forget and go running out there after him." Well, that was Della's formula and it seemed to work. She didn't go! As she kept crying and grieving she grew thinner and her clothes began to hang on her. She looked terrible, but didn't care. I tried to make her eat but she wouldn't.

There was a church social coming up and I talked two days to get her to go and even helped her to buy some new things to wear that fit her. I can tell you honestly that Della at 135 pounds was a whole new better Della than she was at 207 pounds! She was good looking!! And with that big, sweet, innocent, sad smile, she was pretty and the men let her know it! She danced every dance once I got her started, and laughed and laughed and laughed with happiness! Smitty wasn't there, he was probably at the pool hall bragging bout his hold on her. I ain't gonna say a lot about it, but there was a nice man there named Charles . . . and he took to Della like wet takes to water! Soon, they was going out together, being seen a lot. Smitty heard about it. He wanted to come around and save his ego at the same time so he began to come around the house and tell her she had to move out, he needed a place. I know he wanted her to say, "Come on home then," but she didn't. Instead she said, "Give me a month to see what I'm gonna do and how, then I be gone." He didn't really want that house, he wanted Della, but his pride and ego kept him from tellin her. I don't really know what would have happened if he had told her, but anyway, Charlie told her to move in with him, he was buying his own house. She just said she would think about it.

One day Smitty came by to check on his "house" and Charlie was there. Smitty said, blustering, "Well, I'm here now and you better go! This is a husband talkin to his wife and you oughta leave!"

Charlie answered softly, "Well Smitty, I didn't come to see you at your invitation . . . I came to see Della at her invitation, so you can't tell me to go . . . only Della can do that!" Smitty said, taken aback, "This is my house! I say what goes on here! And this is my wife!" Della said softly, "This the landlord's house and I been paying the rent Smitty, so it's not your house." She looked neat and clean and pretty and you could smell the food cooking! Smitty repeated, stubborn, "I want to talk to my WIFE!" Charlie said, just as stubborn, "When she tells me to go, I will!" Della said, "I invited him to supper Smitty, I can't tell my company to go!" Smitty said, "I'm your man, invite me to supper!" Della said back "No . . . you said you wasn't my man, that I was the man. Charlie don't think I'm a man."

Smitty, quick to think wrong, "Why don't he think you a man? What you been doin with him?" He balled his fist up! Charlie put in "I hope to marry Della some day."

Smitty said, "She already married! To me!" They both looked surprised when Della said, "I ain't made up my mind about anything!" She looked thoughtful for a minute then continued, "Charlie will eat supper, then he will go, then you can come back and talk." Smitty was outdone! "Come back?" he asked. Della was up to it. "If you want to!"

So Smitty left, but before he was out the door completely Charlie said, standing in the doorway like it was his, "Smitty, I am interested in Della and she is my friend, so if I leave it ain't so you can do whatever you want to her. Don't hurt her, don't touch her, because I will know about it!" Smitty left mumbling to hisself that wasn't nobody gonna do nothin to him!

Now, all the time I been knowing Della, she always said how Smitty didn't remember no birthday presents or Valentines day or nothing, she always gave him things, but when Smitty came back he was dressed up and had a bag of candy in his right hand and some flowers in his left hand. But he came in fussing, "Ain't you gon offer me no dinner or cake or nothin? Are you just gonna give some to that Charles that don't want nothin but to go to bed with you? Then he gon be gone, just like he done all them other women I done heard of!" Della jumped up and went to get some cake and don't you think Smitty didn't take heart from that! "Sure," she said, "I got plenty cake. You want some coffee?" Smitty leaned back, smiling, "Yes, I would like some coffee, too!"

As he ate the cake, Della was quiet but he talked a lot about how well he was doing. "And I been thinking bout takin a trip, like a vacation!" Della sighed, he went on talking, "Maybe putting some money in this house to make it look a little better!" Della looked around the room and nodded. He smiled and went on "Might even go-head and try to get one of my own!" Della's eyes opened wide and she said "It must be nice to own your own house!" That encouraged him, his chest came out and he decided to play his ace card and hit Della with something that would wake her up and make her realize she didn't want to lose him!

"Della," he said, serious-like in a new deep voice, as he wiped the last cake crumb from the saucer with his finger, "Della, we gon have to do something . . . now . . . or I'm going to get a divorce!" The room was real quiet while Della stared at Smitty, her man for so long.

"You done found somebody else you love, Smitty?"

He laughed. "No, I don't want none of these women that keep running after me! They worry me to death!" He flecked off a speck from his pants as he waited for her to cry out "I don't want no divorce Smitty!" But she didn't. She just sat there staring down at the floor and pretty soon tears came slowly down her cheeks. Smitty saw this and felt his point was won. He stood up and stuck his chest out saying, "Well Della, we can't go on like this . . . I'm a man!" Della looked up and the tears stopped and dried. "I need a wo-man! and if it's gonna be you then say so, if it ain't, then I better get on bout my business and . . . (he leaned toward her) get my divorce!" He waited a moment for her to say the words that would give him his old good life back, but there was only silence, Della looking at the floor again. He straightened up and looked around the home toward the bedroom where he really wanted to go and lay his big pride down. He tried to think of a way to stretch his visit out, but had played his ace too soon, so he cleared his throat and gave himself the next invitation. "I'll be by in a few days to get your answer and I'm gonna come with my bags, Della!" It was said almost like a question.

Della started crying and he went to put his arms around her and rub on her back. "Della, you know I'm your man, now act like you got some sense girl and cut out all this dating and stuff! You my wife and you lucky and he lucky I didn't kick ass this day!" She stepped back from his arms. He continued, "Go wash your face and go to bed, no more company tonight! I'll be back in a few days, Friday, with my bags and get your life back together again cause you acting like a fool!" (Sometimes I wonder about people.) She let him kiss her and then led him to the door and he left feeling good about being a man about the whole thing.

Della didn't sleep much that night and got up saying she "might as well get this over with" and went down town and got a lawyer and filed for a divorce, which takes 30 days in this town, then came home and moved most of her stuff in my house. When Friday came she went over and sat on a chair right in front of the door and waited for Smitty. He came grinning in with his suitcase without knocking and she handed him the papers saying, "This what you want Smitty, if you want it, it must be right! But I like married life so I'm gonna be marrying up with Charles when this is final. I done moved so here is your house ... now, I'll be going!!" He cussed her again but didn't try to hit her and he told her "I don't want this house, ain't nothin' in it!" She left first, then he did and the next day she moved all her stuff back in it!

She was true to her word. When the divorce was final, the marriage plans was made. I wondered about all that so I ask her, "Don't you think you rushin into one marriage after another?" She always takes her time to answer. "No ... ," she said, "I really done learned a lot. I have learned in these few months when I been workin on a job and workin this stuff out with Smitty. I know bout cookin and not havin to cook. I know about a peaceful house when you alone in it ... havin your own money or waiting for somebody to bring you some ... and sleepin alone, or with a husband! My life ain't never gonna be like it was before ... ever again! But ... I like havin a husband, I want a man of my own!" So the marriage plans went on.

I was just sitting at home sewing and wondering about people when about two days before the little wedding, Della came running and screaming over to my house, tears streaming down, she was what you call hyster . .rical! She couldn't say a word, just screaming "Smitty," so I followed her over to her house. Smitty was hanging from that same rafter he was always going to hang Della from, looked like he had kicked the chair over. Me, I believe it was an accident and that chair fell over. I think he was either trying to fix it so Della would catch him in time to stop him and realize she loved him, or he was fixin it for her and the chair fell over! Anyway, he was hanging there dead. I took her home and called Charles and he took care of everything, like a man. She didn't have to do anything except sign some papers for the insurance. She wanted to put the wedding off but Charles wouldn't have none of that!! And all those range-ments made too!!

They got married and she moved into her new home. It's been a year or so now and they seem happy and peaceful and Della is gainin her weight back, up to 200 pounds and just as happy as she can be. Sometimes when she gets to thinking bout Smitty, she says "I still blieve if I had been there, he wouldn't have done that. He would have used me instead and we'd all be alive today!" I tell her, "Better for that fool to accidentally kill hisself like a fool than for you to be a fool and let him kill you!" Sometimes I wonder bout Della!!

Color Me Real

IT DOES not matter what year it was or where, it would have been just as terrible and tragic at any time. Minna, a 13 year-old child, was seduced by a grown white man her mother worked for. She had a man child that he never recognized. A year later she had a girl child by the same seducer. It would seem strange and suspect, this second child, except that money, that old cross, was almost non-existent in the child-mother's family and she was trying to get money for food from the babies' father and he gave it to her "on condition". Minna was in need. Her whole family was hungry. Her last intention was to sell her body, but the whole world knows what can happen to the best intentions in a mother's mind when it comes to her hungry child, a hungry, sickly grandmother, brothers and sisters lining the cold hearth and empty cupboard. An empty coal bin results in a cold stove. Few things are worse than four or five hungry people alternately staring at and looking away from the others that hold no answers, only needs.

By rights, money was owed them by this particular white man for work done for him, but he had decided to hold off paying. His intent was to have Minna again. After the first time he had seduced her he thought she would cease holding off in her child-like fear and come sleep in his cold lonely bed, but she did not. So he added hatred to his lust for her. He made his plan and did not pay Minna's mother, nor Minna for helping her, the cooking and cleaning pay for two months. He locked his cupboard and coal bin and everything else they could use or sell, then sat back, picking his teeth and belching after his dinner. He ate at the little greasy "Addies Eats" diner and gave them just enough for one person to eat and sat and watched them fix it so they would have none in his absence. He watched them grow nervous, hungry and afraid, but he did not see the anger. I don't know why. His power blinded him, I guess.

He kept them there, working, by saying his money was held up and he would be getting it any day now and would pay. They knew he lied, at least they thought so, but what could they do? The judge and the sheriff were white. So Minna was forced to take her baby boy over to him to ask for help. Money she had already earned. He tied the little boy gently to a wicker chair. The white-skinned child with his own face was his child, he thought, as he finished tying him and patted him on the head. He then lay Minna down on the bed and rode her all morning into the afternoon. The baby, tired from crying, had fallen asleep, head hanging over the ropes tied around him by his father, his gasping breaths jerking his little body as he slept, crying out now and again without even waking up. The second baby, a girl named Era, was born nine months later. During that nine months the sickly grandmother moved out into the woods she knew so well and picked her herbs and roots and puttered over them silently and somehow they found their way into the white man's house and somehow he became blind which was soon followed, somehow, by impotency. But they, Minna's family, were kind to him. They continued to care for him and they never had to wait for their money again because they had to do everything for him that involved money. They never cheated him, but he never cheated them again either. He tried to get a wife once, so he could get rid of them. He suspected something, but could not be sure of what. No white woman wanted a blind, impotent husband though, so he remained single and they remained to take care of him in his time of need.

Time passed and the children were growing. Minna worked in the schoolhouse in exchange for letting her children sit in the back of the room to get a general education, and insisted they go even with all the taunts, teasings and insults they received there from the other children. An older brown-skinned playmate, George, was companion and protector to Era. He lived up the road and was never far from her, going to and from school.

When Era was about 17 years old, George said he would marry her, but she really didn't see George. Her brother had been running off and coming back home for the past two or three years bringing tales of a bigger and better life. One day while cleaning her father's room, Era went into a box of his cash kept under his mattress and took $400. Packing her few things in a cardboard box, she got George, now working, to drive her to town and left on the bus that came through town headed for New York, checked into the YWCA and signed up for secretarial school. She had a plan in mind. When she had graduated, near the top of her class, she moved on to Idlewild, where, her brother had told her, the rich men were idle and the women were wild!

Era was a good-looking woman and she chose to pass for white because it would make her way easier, and she planned to get ahead in life and get a wealthy husband to take care of her. She loved her family at home and planned to send them things and be good to them, but her greatest fear was of being as hungry as she had been at some times in her life. She remembered doing without the smallest things that sometimes make a big difference in daily life.

Well, Era got a job at a brokerage firm and in two years or so had married one of the clients there. He was not rich but he was on his way. She couldn't invite her mother and family to the wedding. She wrote them about it!

They had a good life for several years. Then, while on a two-day shopping trip in New York, Era got sick and left her friends to come home. When she arrived, she found her husband in her bed with a black woman! Her husband admired her tolerance and understanding attitude toward the black woman and offered her to share, but both black women refused the offer. The black woman was sent away in a cab.

Era was silent and thoughtful because she was hurt. She had loved her husband.

To make a long story short, when they were getting into the freshly cleaned bed, he held Era and kissed her through her tears and made many declarations of love, true love, deepest love . . . and said he didn't know what it was about black women that he liked so much. Just always had! But that they would never compare to her and so on and on. Era let her logic carry her away and she told him, "If what you really want is a black woman, then you have one. I am a black woman." He stared at her a few moments then laughed and told her she didn't have to go that far! Era got up and got pictures her mother had sent her over the years, saying, "This is my mother." She smiled at him and the photos. He snatched the photographs and stared at them until he dropped them to the floor. When he turned to her his fist came with him and he beat the wife, a moment ago he had loved truly, deeply. He refused to have a black woman for a wife so he settled some money on her in the divorce and she left the years she had made a life there, behind her, and flew home to her mother.

Her mother, Minna, still lived in the broken-down little house. Grandmama was dead and gone. Brother was home at the time but living with a woman at the woman's home.

The first thing Era did was buy her mother a better house closer in to the little town and they made a home of it. She stayed there about a year. George had already moved to town and had his own business as a gardener. He had remained single and was taking care of his mother.

Now, Era was a simple uncomplicated woman, born and raised around growing things and animals, trees and space. These things still pleased her, so George would take her to work with him sometimes to break the monotony for her, but still she didn't really see him. He worked with her in her own yard and it became one of the best. George loved his work and his flowers blossomed in all the wealthier white folks' yards. He was reliable and smiled a lot. They liked that, so he prospered. Era took pleasure also in reading to her mother and dressing her in good clothes. She did her hair and gave her facials for fun.

As Minna improved in looks and confidence, several older gentlemen, who at first came to look upon Era, began to turn their faces to this quiet, shy woman who hadn't had much of anything. Not friends, laughter or male companionship. Minna blossomed and soon became attached to one pleasant man, Arthur. Era stayed until her mother's first and only wedding. The only bad part of the day was when brother beat his black woman after the wedding reception. Later, when he took Era to the station to leave, she stood on the train steps and asked him if he thought he was white, and if that was why he beat his darker-hued wife whom he said he loved? And why didn't he marry her? Because of his daddy? "Well," she continued (before he could answer, because the train was pulling out), "that white man who raped our mama was not just a white man, he was a child molesting, raping, ignorant, slimy, cruel bastard . . . who died alone! Is that who you think you are?"

"At least I ain't try'n to pass for white!" he hollered back at her as the train was gathering a little speed.

"No!" she shouted back at him, "You tryin to pass for a

man!" Then the train was too far away to answer her so they watched each other until the track curved and they could not.

Era chose Chicago this time and after becoming settled, finding work, looked around for something "meaningful" to do. She volunteered to help in a political campaign for a black man. The headquarters was always full of many people including lawyers and other politicians. Some bringing something to give, some coming to get something. Now Era was black, and that was that in her mind. However, quite a few men took her to be white. Consequently she had quite a few lunch dates, which she thought was normal. One in particular, Reggie, began to show up when he didn't have to be there. He often told her, "You are my kind of woman!" Which goes to show you everybody can take the same set of words and all go off in their own direction as to what those words mean! Dinner dates were soon added to lunch dates; then cocktails and dancing.

Reggie liked all the attention Era got, the admiring glances from the other lawyers and professional men. Since it is rather obvious to you he was rather shallow, it will stand to reason if I tell you he soon proposed. One night he had the ring, the license, the car and the gas and he drove a few counties away, convincing Era all the way of his love for her and how far they would go together. She married him because she thought he was not exactly a fly-by-nighter. He was part of a good law firm, had a nice home (where the bar was filled but the pantry empty), and a boat. The marriage went pretty well the first year or two. But Era discovered her black husband thought she was white, and it seemed so important to him she didn't tell him the truth right then and later it became harder to tell. But here was another man, a black man, she could not take home to her mother . . . yet.

The decision was made one night when he had the fellows, those who had white wives, over to his house for cocktails and the conversation came naturally around to the kind of women black women were. Era was a little tired of going into the kitchen or getting busy somewhere else when these conversations came up, so she just listened and thought. She knew from conversations with the white wives that most of them felt superior to their black men and one of their fantasies was to picture them, during lovemaking, as slaves; the black skin glistening on the white skin helped multiple orgasms along. So when the black men ridiculed their own black women, saying, among other things, "Black women are not ready, never had been ready and it would take 10,000 more years before the sister would begin to get ready," the white women smiled, because they knew it was against the rules to laugh out loud at black women in these meetings in front of the other black brothers. But they moved to the kitchen or bedroom and, passing each other, the thrill in their hearts showed in their eyes as they looked at each other.

Era was setting a dish of hors d'oeuvres on the table when her husband said, "Black women will never stop castrating their men and when I have a son, I'm going to tell him, 'Son, don't be a fool and marry a black woman, get one just like your mama!'"

Era, full of it all, interrupted, "Reggie, do I castrate you?" He patted her on the hip and laughed, "Baby, we not talking about you all, we are talking about black women," then he looked around for accord from his black brothers. Era didn't laugh.

"Which one of you black brothers got a white mama?" She spoke quietly. "If you don't have a white mama, then it's your own mother you are dragging in mud, all the women in your families who carry the same blood you do!"

Reggie stopped smiling and looked seriously at Era, "Listen," he started to say something.

Era looked around the room at the men, "When you was growin up, who tried to starve you and who tried to feed you? And when you find a foot in your behinds, now that

71

you are grown, what color is it?" Era threw the plate of food against the wall over the record player and it fell on the turn-table and knocked the needle off the Miles Davis record and began to spin and knock against the boards. Reggie jumped up to quiet his wife, acutely conscious of what the others were seeing and hearing, "Baby, baby!"

Then she said, "I am a black woman! I never told you I was white. I knew you didn't want to hear that!"

Reggie stiffened, "I don't want to hear it now!"

But Era didn't care anymore. "What's so big about you, so grand, that you think you aren't stooping down when you try to tear black women down, women your own color? What makes you think you can tear half a thing down and leave the other half up? You weren't freed from slavery any earlier than she was!"

Reggie reached for her but she moved away, still talking.

"I'm gonna tell you something. Black women don't care if you like white women. What we really resent, and what makes us so disgusted with you, is that you have to stand on our shoulders, tear us down, make us look like nothing to make yourself big enough to do what you want to do! Just go on and like em if you want to, only stop tearing us down to do it! Some white women are really alright! So, it's O.K.!"

Reggie was beyond anger. His male friends saw that and rounded up their coats and wives, who were trying to remember all the things they had told Era when they thought she was white. They left.

Reggie beat Era, lawyer or not, pushed her down the stairs so she could see the front door and said, "See that door, black bitch? You be gone out of it when I get back here in a few days." Then he tore her clothes off her and made evil love to her as hard as he could. When he was finished, bitten and scratched, he grabbed his boat keys and left, saying, "I don't want you no more!"

Era lay there and cried and cried until it was far into the night. She wasn't crying for the loss of Reggie or the nice

house or the boat. It was the loneliness. She wanted someone to love her and she wanted to love someone . . . real. She
called an ambulance, stayed two days in the hospital, where,
fortunately, she learned nothing was broken. Came out,
packed her things, went to a lawyer, stopped downtown and
charged a new wardrobe for the country. Mailed back the
charge cards to her husband with a note saying, "The cards
come back from the black side, the bills will come from the
white side of me." Then she drove home to her mother's to
recuperate and think about her life and what she was going
to do next.

Everything was still the same at home, quiet and peaceful,
seeming far removed from big city racing. George was still
there and they worked in the garden again and when Era
needed something more to fill the days, she would go with
George to work on his jobs. She liked being out in the sun,
working in the earth. Sometimes they talked.

"George, you are still doing exactly the same things every
time I come home."

"What I'm going to change for? It suits me! Don't give me
no black eyes and big bruise!"

Silence would follow. But another time, she would say,
"You know, you could make more money. Get a bigger
house!"

"I'm doin alright! Do what I want to do! You can't always
buy the things you want, you know." He would smile.

Silence. Then George might say, as he put the flower
bulbs gently into the ground, "You had a big house . . . twice,
far as I know. What they do for you?"

Era would pat the earth down gently around the bulb,
"You know what I mean, George."

Another time. "George, why haven't you married? Had
children?"

"Era, I'm gonna marry the woman I love. I don't love
them women I fool with!"

"Who do you fool with, George?"

He stood up. "This is a small kinda town ... so when I need a woman, I gets dressed and go up the highway to a nice place I know and spend my money and when I get back, that's all there is to it! Not nobody gonna be knockin on my door worryin me!"

"Ain't nothing wrong with marriage, George. You need to be married!" She looked up at him.

He bent back to his work, "Ain't done you no good, Era!"

Silence again. Off and on they talked about all the things they felt and thought about life. George was a little deeper than Era had thought, and she found she was not as deep as she thought she was!

Another time. "George, my marriages were different. I tried to make them both work."

"What went wrong then?" He was digging around a tree.

"I was too black, George."

"What that mean, Era?"

"Well," she said thoughtfully, "One husband needed what he did not want ... the other husband wanted what he did not need."

George stopped digging and looked at Era. "Was you wanting a rich man? How come they picked you?" He picked up the shears and began pruning the tree, spreading the lowered branches apart so he could look at her. She began to drag the branches into a pile, the sunlight blazing down on her now shining, healthy, sun-baked face and body.

She finally answered, "Well, I guess I did, I do. And them? Well they looked at me and each one saw what he needed to see!"

George lowered his head through the branches, "And you helped them see what they wanted to see?"

"Ain't nothing to say but I guess I did!"

"Era, you ain't always sposed to see what you doing, you sposed to feel it! Seem like all you all did was for the look of things."

"George, how come you know so much about it? You have never been married!"

"But I been in love a long, long time, Era."

"Well," her voice seemed strangled somehow, "Why don't you marry her? What's wrong with her?"

As he spoke, everything seemed to become still, suspended in space. "I love you, Era. Always have. Look like I always will. But you not sposed to know that, cause I ain't gonna do a damn thing about it! Ain't got no room for no big heartaches in my life . . . done had one all my life already."

Era's throat tightened and she could feel her own blood rushing through her body while at the same time the sun seemed to blaze brighter and she had to close her eyes from the glare.

Silence again. The rest of the afternoon they said things like, "You want this?", "No, hand me that."

When George called Era the next morning, she said she didn't believe she would go with him. She expected him to come running by that evening; he didn't. Nor the next, nor the next. She drove by his jobs and when she saw him and waved, he smiled. She could see his house from her porch and when he saw her, he waved, smiled and kept right on going about his business. On the week-end she saw him wash and shine his car all afternoon. Later he came out clean and dressed-up. He waved, got in his car and drove off, to the highway.

Era sat on the porch, thinking and staring at George's house far into the night til he came home, then she went in to bed and stared at the ceiling, feeling. Another week went by. He came by and ran in with some flowers for Minna and grabbed Era by the back of the neck, "Seem like I done lost my helper, Ms. Minna!"

Minna answered, "I don't know why! She ain't doin nothin round here cept reading and lookin out the window and sittin on that porch!"

George let go Era's neck, "Well, people got to read and

look out windows too. I got to go!"

Minna asked, "What's your hurry? Stay and have some supper, Era cooked it."

"No, ma'm," George smiled. "Got to get home and clean up. Going to hit the highway this evenin!" He started out the door.

Era spoke sarcastically, "Again? You sure hitting the highway a lot!"

He smiled at her, "How you FEELING, Ms. Era?" He put a lot into that word "Feeling".

"You ain't been calling 'Ms. Era', call me Era!"

He smiled at her as he got into his truck, "Era, you sound like you don't feel too good." He drove away.

She didn't have to wait on the porch as long this time. He was back after a couple of hours. She started across the street to talk to him. For some reason she was angry. But she changed her mind when she realized she didn't have anything really to say. She went back home to bed. She lay there listening to Minna and Arthur talking and laughing in their bedroom. They made things seem so simple, close and good. Where was her man, the man she could live with in peace and love . . . and reality? She thought hard about herself.

The next day she was up early and dressed in her cutest shorts outfit. She went and worked in the garden. When George passed, she smiled and waved him by. For a week she did her yard and helped the neighbors on each side of her, in a new cute shorts outfit every day. She seemed to perk up each time George's truck came by and he seemed to find more reasons to come home for a minute. On the week-end, when he had cleaned his car and himself and was driving away, he slowed in front of Era's house where she was painting the fence.

"Good lord! you are busy Era! You gon paint the house next?"

"If I FEEL like it!"

"That's right!" He smiled, "Always try to do what you feel! Wait for the feeling!"

Era placed her hands on her hips. "You sure feel like hitting that highway a lot!" She screamed at him as he drove away.

He was back early, hardly over an hour. As he parked in his driveway, Era burst through the porch door, slammed it and with her face set, strode across the street toward his house. He saw her coming and held up his hand and strode to meet her, calling, "I'll meet you half way!"

They met in the middle of the road.

They were both silent for a time, then George spoke; his voice was soft in the dusky evening on the empty road.

"What's the matter, girl?"

"I don't know, man!" Her voice, angry, trembled.

"Want to talk about it, woman?"

"Yes . . . " She looked up at him. He took her hand, pulling her toward his house. "Wanta sit down?" He asked.

"I want to know if you meant it when you said you loved me?"

"Yes, I meant it. I also meant I don't want no problems."

"Am I a problem to you, George?"

"Do you love me, Era?"

"I want you . . . is that love? I feel you! Is that love?"

"Sometimes."

"Well, what do you want from me, George?"

"Love . . . and a peace of mind."

"How will we know we'll always feel this way? What will I get from you, George?"

"Love . . . and a peace of mind."

"But how do you know?"

"Because I FEEL it, Era. Always have, always will."

They drew close, standing there for a time, then they kissed for the first of many loving and peaceful times.

She was neither white nor black now. She was a woman, his woman. It lasted til death did them part, leaving beautiful brown children on the beautiful brown earth. They worked their garden which grew abundantly and had mostly . . . love and a peace of mind.

Too Hep to be Happy!

MY NAME is Mrs. Eustace B. (for Bernard) Walker and I am Ida R. Walker, myself. I have lived in this house, this same house!, for 81 years! I was born here, raised here, married here and I lived right here! My sisters and brothers all moved away and left me early on. I have done my duty by everybody . . . I stayed here. First, my father died, then my mother passed and last of all, my husband passed. Oh yes! I stayed and done my duty and . . . still doing it! I am 81 years old and don't know if I did my duty to myself right or not; but I can't change nothin now. But when you live that long to be that age, you have done something right! Least ways if you look good as I do! Everybody says I look good! Ain't no need for them to lie!

Sit on down over there. Make yourself comfortable. I'm gonna roll out these rolls and pop them in the oven for us to make our acquaintance by. I'm a good cook!

Now, up and down this street, you know I have seen it grow from a path, to a road, to a street, with rocks and mud and horses, to gravel and finally that ugly black tar for cars. I rather horses myself! I rather smell horse manure than spend good money on gas that just blows out and it's gone. But anyway, back to what I'm trying to tell you.

Now where's my flour?

I sees most everything, if not everything that goes on in this here town, and all I don't see, I blieve I hear about! I mean I hear it all! But I like what I can see, cause I can count on that! You can't count on what people say ... now can you? They say what they think they saw. But when you see, then you see! Now, what I done seen, for all kinds of years 20, 30, 40, 50, 70 and 80 headin toward 90, then a hundred, I hope! Don't you?

These rolls are going to be delicious!

Now on this street, there be eight or nine families; for all the years I have been here. In most of em the daddy done died or gone, most all the grammas and grampas and even some of the kids. But I notice the wives get left behind more. That's why so many women alone in this town and that's why these women that got men got to hold on to em, cause most of these church goin folks here don't mind taken your husband or your wife for a while anyway ... That's what brings me to the very person I want to tell you about. Mr. Luther Lester! L.L.!

Now, there have been all kinds of women, sick ones, well ones, even one blind one have liked that man! He is old now, or older I guess is a better word. He bout 70 years old or so. But he always been kinda nice and soft and easy going; least ways it seemed like he was. He always seem to be givin you somethin! But, it all be second hand trash from the junk yard, stuff that still works a little. Still if you ain't got one, and he got a used one to give you ... what you gonna do? Do you know? See what I mean, chile? So he give away a lot, been given to him, don't cost him a dime! And if it do, he gets that much from you by way of a piece of chicken or a piece of pie, half a cake or a ham hock or two!

I don't know is he a lover or not cause we ain't never crossed the same road together! My husband was alive and his friend for bout 50 years (now he dead, rest his soul, he was a good man, you know), and Lester used to come over here and talk and drink beer and I used to hear them talk. If I didn't hear them talk, my husband would tell me later, cause I kept my mouth shut. I learned early that you learned more if your mouth was shut! Before and after! So you can tell me anything you want to bout your business cause I'll take it to my grave with me. I don't tell nothin!

Now, let me finish tellin you. Luther Lester never was married. No! Not ever! Got all he needed of everything without marrying up with nobody. These ladies done killed they selves off on account of losing all the power . . . in the give-away! You can't give away nothin worth something! Do, sometime it means it wasn't worth much. Course that means did you give it to a fool or not! But it seem to me . . . and I may be dumb, cause I ain't been here but 81 years . . . that he liked all of em! Even the sick ones . . . so he can feel like he givin them something. All of em! Well . . . 70 years . . . you got time to get em all! Well . . . me, myself . . . I think he takes somethin away.

How many ain't so important no way . . . it's the fact and reason he ain't never kept nobody for his own! He been nice to em all, but ain't never spent a long dime . . . maybe a short one for a beer or somethin, but not a long one, like for nothin they need that might have to be brand new. You know what I mean?

Ohhh these rolls are turning out nicely.

I didn't really pay that man no real mind until my niece came here to stay awhile and it come to my attention to think about him. She was right pretty, wasn't too young and wasn't old, but was real nice. A real nice person. Had a city name, Rayetta; one of them sisters of mine done dug a trench in the city and stayed there. She, Rayetta, had pretty hair and skin and legs and a powerful bust and behind; you know the kind. Men likes them same now as a thousand years ago, I guess. Anyway, she came and she was always walkin, goin somewhere, and a whole lot of men got to see her, and the women, too. (*I'm gonna put this pan in the oven.*) Well, Lester commence to coming round askin me if I needed anything and how was I and all that . . . you know what I mean? And his eyes just bulge out and around corners and all, to get a look at Rayetta. She thought it was cute in a amusin kind of way so she encouraged him by laughin and talkin with him and having a beer or two. He was 70 years old, for God's sake! What he wanta be sniffin round somebody for? I thought to myself, what could he do, do he get her in that position? But whatever he could do . . . he sure wanted to try it! Then, he got to taken her for a ride in that ole grey jalopy of his! All that money he got (oh, he got plenty money), and he won't buy a decent automobile. They would ride bout a hour or so, she say the car make so much noise you couldn't hear no conversation so they just bounced all over these country roads! Then he bring her back, grinning. She just laugh . . . not mean, just havin fun.

Now somehow, she got to thinking nobody ever done much for him and she like to see people happy so she start to takin cakes and pies over to his house and little things she pay money for, given them to him and he took them all . . . grinning. But he don't never give her nothin but a beer. Then, I guess he wondered what he could do (in the bed) if she was to let him. She say he was always tryin to feel her bust on the secret, you know what I mean? (My husband used to do that to women sometime . . . damm him!) She was mostly just laughin, but somethin happened and she took to takin special care for her looks when she was going to see him! And sitting round that phone when it didn't ring! And it got to where he didn't call or even come by sometimes! I could see that woman was likin on that man . . . really!!! I don't know what he done, but he knew somethin to do. Cause she start talkin bout maybe she would live here. Live here! And wonderin why he ain't never been married and why he was alone. I coulda told her he wasn't alone . . . he had a married woman he been goin with for years . . . but I didn't want to tell her somethin that would make her think she liked him for sure! She was already sayin he wasn't happy and his house needed cleaning and all. (I just was watchin cause I thought I must be learning somethin new but I didn't never find out what it was.)

Now that good lookin, young woman became that old man's lover! You understand me? Do you understand? I don't know how many times, but once is enough! Whatever he did, he musta done it right! I ask her if she knew what she was doing thinkin like that bout a old man. She said, "He may be old, but he was a good man, a honest man, reliable, kind, sweet, always kept his word," stuff like that! Well I said to myself she had some sense to like a man like that, cause it was all true.

I thought like that til I went to bed that night and my mind could see through the dark to the truth and it hit me in the middle of my head that he was all those things . . . BUT a person can think you good cause they don't know nothin bout you if you keeps your business to yourself! You can be honest, if you ain't poor and don't want nothing; new car, clean house, nothin! Reliable, if you don't promise nobody nothin but little bitty things don't take no time nor money, and kind, if you just smile and say nice things cause you ain't givin nobody nothing that would make you mad if you don't get it back. There was two sides to that coin and he was on both sides. Kept his word cause he never gave it if a thing was too big! I was proud of myself too, cause I had done some real thinkin! I was havin fun doing it too! I planned to tell Rayetta about it all, but before I got a chance to they musta talked bout marriage and he told her he was already happy. Chile, that 70 year-old man dropped that young fine woman, smart from the city! Well, didn't drop her . . . he do anything she ask if she don't ask too much. Wasn't long before Rayetta laughed a little broken laugh and went on back home to the big city to people she could understand.

Just a little more time now our rolls be ready! I blieve I'll send Lester some of these.

Anyway, where was I? Oh, at the end! Anyway, that Lester rambled round in my mind after she left. I thought to myself: He ain't happy (or is he?) Ain't nobody happy, ain't spozed to be, if they are alone! He ain't got chick or child to worry bout or leave all that money and property to. Just sittin on it! He close to dyin... sure ain't gon get no younger! Rayetta was fun, clean, cooked nice, drank beer with him and all without being a drunk. I can't stand a drunk woman! And he didn't want her!

Well, when he came by one day (to ask about her, I could tell), I sat out on the porch and gave him some cake and lemonade and we talked. I looked him over real good and he wasn't bad at all in his body, so I tried lookin in his mind. Now it ain't no sense in beatin round the bush with the fellow who planted it so I said right out, "How come you ain't never married, Lester?" He chewed awhile, lookin in his plate then up to the sky and finally said, "I blieve if you doin alright you ought to keep it thata way!"

I said, "Spose you could do better if you change?"

He grinned, "That's somethin we don't know, least I don't know."

I pushed, "Nobody know til they try!"

He said, "Well Mz. Walker, when I was growen up, my mama always fighten with my daddy til he left. I don't want that."

He thought that would shut me up. I went further, "Every woman ain't your mama!"

He grinned. "That's right. Every woman ain't my mama." Then he didn't say nothing so I pushed on. "Seems to me a person would want to try something if he old enough to know what he's doing." I wanted to say something mean about his being a old fool but that's as far as I could fix it.

He said, "Yea, if he know what he's doing."

I could see he was as far as he was going so I said, "And if

84

he meet a nice person, who makes him happy, he ought to try to keep that happiness."

Grinning again, he said, "Yea, a person sure should try to keep the happiness he finds."

Now I understood part of his secret; see, he only gives you back what you give him . . . no more . . . so it's like you talkin to yourself and he says it always with a smile so you got to think he nice! You understand? But I wanted more so I said, "Mr. Lester, you old enough now not to be afraid of life. You ain't got nothin to lose by livin it til you die."

He said (smiling), "Sure got to live it til I die."

I said, "Oh shit! Mr. Lester, can't you think for yourself?"

He looked at me. "I do . . . I think for myself . . . and I blieve I know what you gettin to."

So I told him, "Well, get to it then!"

He said, "Mz. Walker, I am an old man!"

I said, "You wasn't always old! You didn't get married when you was 20 either!"

He said, "I was too poor."

I said, "Well, you worked and got you some money and property, then what?"

He said (no smile), "Well, then I knew nobody wasn't gonna want me just for myself! They gonna want my house or my money."

I said, "That's what you think of all the women was foolin with you?" Somehow his guard or somethin dropped cause he snapped, "That's right! I ain't never known a woman that wasn't a huzzy deep down in her heart! Womens is danger-ous! They lie! They ain't got a serious bone in their body! They just want to dance, laugh and spend money. They are greedy people who want to come out the kitchen and sit like a lady in the livinroom! I ain't gon let none of em make a fool of me! They woulda spent MY money on clothes and cars and furniture and trips and whatever all that women find to spend money on!" He wore himself out and clicked them foolish false teeth. I should have snatched em from his mouth and crushed em for lettin such words pass through em!

I whispered to him, "Some of those things might have made life worth living more."

He whispered back, "Yea . . . theirs!"

I said (I could hardly believe I didn't shut up and put him off my porch, but I was learning something), "Didn't you meet some nice women in your church?"

He grinned, "Yes ma'm! Some nice women."

I said, "Well? What about them?"

He said (with great pleasure), "While the lord was askin for my soul, they was askin for my pole! Scuse me ma'm, but you asked!"

I said, "You didn't turn nobody down."

He said, "I like to see folks happy! Some folks."

I went on, feelin foolish myself, "But you didn't want them to be too happy so you didn't marry them, huh?"

He looked at me. "Lord knows, I don't know nobody happy that's been married—ceptin your husband (he remembered) and I don't want none of that kinda life for myself."

I couldn't shut up. "I don't know nobody happy who is single."

He told me, "People don't love people . . . they use people! I ain't gonna be used! I was smart enough to get what I got and I'm gonna be smart enough to keep it!"

I said, "It's more to life than money!"

He said, "What?"

I said, "Love, being together, helpin each other."

He said, "Yea that's what everybody want . . . help!" He stood up to go. I said, "You too smart for that, huh?"

He said, "Yea, like they say in the city . . . I am hep!" He laughed one of them cackling laughs that old men make when they think they said something smart. I knew then what his trouble was. I knew Rayetta and nobody else would have been happy WITH him. He gave no more than he received and sometimes not as much. Yes, I knew the answer. He was "hep" as they say in the city.

He went on down the stairs, all alone, smiling and talkin. I don't know what he said cause I was lookin at him and thinkin bout him. He got into his raggity car, all alone, and when it didn't start he got out, smiling, and lifted the hood and did something that started the car, all alone. Lookin up at me and waving good-by, all alone, and drove slowly down to the corner, all alone, and pulled into HIS driveway, all alone, and stepped out of the car, walked slowly up the path to HIS door, all alone, and went in, all alone. All alone in his dirty, junky house filled with second hand stuff that he don't want to share with nobody.

NOW! Let's you and me butter up some of these nice hot rolls and get a piece of that crispy hot chicken and some of that gravy! There's some ice-cold lemonade in the ice box . . . and let's eat!

Later on, maybe . . . I'll fix up a few rolls for Mr. Lester cause I feel sorry for him and he can take them home and eat em, all alone. I don't let him sit here with me anymore; let him be alone, alone. Maybe I will, maybe I won't . . . cause you know what I think? Lester's happiness depends a lot on what other people do for him . . . more than he knows. He is hep . . . TOO HEP TO BE HAPPY!

Lord! Ain't these rolls good! My Lord! Have some more chile!

The Free and the Caged

THIS story started somewhere else until I discovered it had two beginnings, so I had to tell you this one also.

Having raised two children—a man and a woman now— and been married thirty years to the same man, Vilma was tired, tired, tired. She was far gone.

Her son, though raised as upper middle class and given every advantage such as college, etc, had chosen street corners, dope and wine and unemployment. She had to watch him when he came to the house because she knew he needed money and he would steal it from her and if not *it*, then something to get *it* with.

Her daughter, having the same advantage, chose to love someone, or several someones, who gave her babies, three now, all different colors. They had left her and she was being subsidized by the government each month. She often brought the kids to stay with their grandmother so she could go out and try to get another one that she would surely bring over in some future time. Vilma loved her grandchildren, but she was tired, tired, tired.

Then her husband, having his own little business that did

quite well, had plenty time to fool around with other women, and this he did. Their sex life was out there in the
street, left behind him at some other woman's house. So
Vilma was tired. Tired of the cooking, washing, cleaning,
and shopping and paying bills and Christmas dinners, she
cooked, Thanksgiving dinners she cooked and cleaned up
after, everybody else gone off with their happy asses and
she, mama, left alone in the middle of a mess of mess.

Consequently, though Vilma believed in God, she didn't
believe in Him enough for it to hold her together. Because
she had heard so many loose-living people put the Bible
down, she wasn't sure, so she turned to other things like
alcohol, cigarettes, pills for sleeping and best of all, books.
But she was looking like hell about now. Too much alcohol
was ruining her face, her skin, eyes and, well, it's really
poison, you know.

One day, Vilma got hold of one of these Bible aid books
and, reading it, she realized she had always known, just
never realized: her children were way past old enough to be
responsible for themselves and had made all their own
choices and she was not called upon to be there to hold a
place for them to use when they needed it, and that her
husband was an adulterer and she did not have to stay with
him and suffer in this way.

It took about two weeks for Vilma to get her head clear
and turn daydreams into plans (she noticed that with every
plan her need for alcohol was less and soon she didn't even
need sleeping pills). Vilma went down to the lawyer's and
filed for divorce and went home. They advertised in
another state for him because they didn't know him, you
know how a big city is, and after all the legalities were over,
she went to court and got her divorce granted, though her
husband never knew. Then she went to the bank and put
half the money in an account of her own, traded her automobile, a new one with payments, on an older one with no
payments—a little convertible so she could see more and

not feel caged in. Packed her bag, wrote a note telling her ex-husband he could stay there until he heard from her, sent a copy to her lawyer. Then, hitting the highway, she decided to follow the sunrise, and did! The next year she followed the sunset and that's where this other story begins.

*   *   *

The sound came before the car did and Jacob kept right on pruning his trees. Cars and people didn't pass here often, but when they did, so what! He had his business to tend to. When the sound stopped in front of his house, he didn't look up right away, just sighed and straightened up and looked toward the place where the sound had been.It was a neat little convertible with a new looking older woman in it. She smiled and the angels kind of sang.

"Evening!" She waved.

"Evening!" He returned as he wondered what she was doing on this road. It was off the main road and was seldom used. Since his wife had died two years ago and his son had moved to the city, there were few visitors.

"May I have some water, please? My car is hot and dry and I am hot and dry!" She smiled again.

"Sure." He put down his pruning tool. "But you betta leave it running if you gonna put water in it!"

"Oh! She'll be alright! I treat her right, she treats me right! Where's the water?"

"You want inside water or outside water? Got a well round back." He pointed up the driveway.

"Outside water, well water!" she smiled.

"Where you heading?" he asked as they walked toward the back of the fine old house through a clean orderly yard.

"Everywhere and nowhere!" She bounced the words over her shoulder.

"I mean, now?" he asked again, pleasantly.

"I do, too! I'm only here because I was following the sunset, it was so lovely and it's almost gone, then the car got hot and dry and, you know the rest!" she ended as they reached the well. She helped herself, handling the bucket easily.

"Yeah, these days are hot!" he admitted.

"Hmmm, hmmm," she agreed drinking water from the dipper.

"These nights are hot, too," he mused, then realized she was a woman and really looked at her body for the first time. She was small-boned, but not thin. He guessed she was in her late forties or early fifties. Casual but neat, hair plainly pulled back and clipped, nice around her makeup-less face. She saw him looking and said, "Where's your wife? In the house?"

"In heaven." He looked up toward the sky.

"How you know she's in heaven?"

"She was a good woman, a good person, a good wife. Where your husband?" A hint of humor in his voice.

"In hell, whether he's living or dead!" She put the dipper down. "I just decided to leave."

"Hadda been me, I wouldn't of let you go!" He smiled.

"He didn't 'let' me go, I just did!" She took the water can he handed her.

"A divorce?" he pursued.

"Who cares?" she laughed. "I'm free! For the first time in my life, FREE! And enjoying it! Wanting more of it! I will never bind myself to anything or anybody again!" Her eyes met his as she spoke and he was looking so intently at her, her laughter melted into the breeze. She looked at the sky. "I better hurry, it's getting dark fast!" Turning to go, she noticed the little cottage under the trees.

"Who lives there?" she asked.

"Nobody. My son used to like to stay there. He's gone now living in the city." He slapped at a mosquito flying near her.

"Can I see it? Will I hold you up? You don't have to walk with me, I don't want to keep you from your work." She said all these things as she set the water can down.

"So what?" he answered, smiling and started walking toward it.

It was lovely, shady and cool at the cottage under all these tall pine and fat Sycamore trees, leaves floating here and there, and the sound of huge limbs loaded with leaves waving and rustling in the wind. Vilma looked up for the birds she knew were there and when she found them, she loved the house. It was as simple as that. Sometimes she longed for a home, like this one, away and free like she was, all by itself.

He saw her face and her joy in the cottage and realized he was enjoying her company, any company.

"It's dark," he said, "you going far?"

"I don't know. I'll have to find somewhere to sleep!" Her jubilance returned.

"You like this cottage? Sleep here!"

"Oh, I'd love to!" she cried, "but I can't pay you much."

"So what? Don't pay me nothin!"

She looked him dead in the eye. "Nothing means nothing!"

"So what! House just sitting here. Clean! I'll get you some sheets and you make the bed and brush up a little, it be alright. Ain't nothing gone bother you out here . . . and that ole kerosene lamp is full, give you all the light you need!" He remarked to himself he was sure saying a lot of words.

"I know it, I love it!" She almost clapped her hands, then held herself serious. "But I'm serious. If you don't take the little bit of money I can offer you, there is nothing else I can give you." She looked him straight in the eyes again.

"So what?" He waved his hand at her. "I'd like to have somebody out here again. Maybe you'll stay to breakfast in the morning. I'm a good cook and we can talk some!" He started out the door. "I'll get the sheets and bring you some fresh water."

"I'll get the water!" She did clap her hands. "And I'll get my things out of the car." She went past him. "And don't

92

worry, I'll leave it neat and clean in the morning!"

He laughed at her, rusty laughter, bottom laughter; wherever it came from, it was happy to be let out. Happy laughter. His step picked up. "So what?" he almost shouted.

Vilma locked the door that night with the crude wooden bar but she needn't have bothered, he didn't come near until the next morning and then he was bringing coffee.

"I know how city people like coffee first thing! Your breakfast is on the table, soon as you get there." And he was gone, leaving the coffee on the small steps.

She had slept naked between the country-smelling sheets, now she lay there after getting the coffee and looked out the window at the huge tree trunks, listening to the leaves, the birds and insects, sounds they make early in the mornings. She noticed a spider crawl from a crack to see her better. "Don't worry ole Ms. Spider, I'm not going to bother your home. You leave me alone, I'll leave you alone." The spider sat there a minute more, then decided to believe her and went on back to its business in the crack.

Vilma walked around the little house after she packed her little suitcase again. It was lovely. She patted the house and said, "Thank you for a lovely night!" Then she went in to breakfast.

"Hey?" she called from outside the screendoor.

"Come on in!" he answered.

"Say, I don't know your name," she said as she looked over the neat house, like a woman still lived here, she thought.

"Jacob . . . Jacob Harley," he said softly but proudly.

"Ohhh Weee!" she laughed. "You CAN cook!!!"

"Sure!" he smiled.

"Probably better than me!" She sat down.

"So what? What's better?" He sat hot biscuits on the table beside the ham, scrambled eggs and grits, syrup, jam and yellow watermelon. "What's your name?"

"Vilma."

"Just Vilma?"

"Vilma is all I need."

"Let's say the blessing, one-name Vilma, and let's eat!"

She did and they did, then breakfast was over and she sat there while he did the dishes, telling him what she had seen in her travels.

She told him she had finally seen a mountain and that it was a monument to God, also. She had seen two oceans, the Pacific and the Atlantic. She had seen a mountain made of stone that looked like Cochise might come around it any moment. And how the sky was different in every state. She had seen great trees, which were her favorite, almost, of anything that grew. She had been to museums and seen some of the world's greatest treasures . . . they were treasures, but if she had to choose what to take home with her, well, she would take an ocean, or a mountain, or a tree . . . Then he was through and they walked outside to the backyard and she picked up her suitcase she had left there.

"I cleaned up after myself," she smiled.

"So what?" He put a foot up on a stump and crossed his arms on his knee.

"I really did appreciate last night. Thank you very much."

"Well, what you leavin for then?"

"Enough is enough," she spoke as she contemplated the ground.

"So what? What's enough?" Though smiling, he looked so serious.

"You didn't expect me!" she smiled back.

"So what?" He sure could look at a person hard.

"So, I'm taking up your time!" She tried to keep smiling and felt the heat of the sun on her teeth.

"So what?" He wouldn't let up at all.

"Is that all you know how to say? So what?" She was uncomfortable. She started walking away.

"If you ain't going nowhere special or don't know where you going, why don't you stay in that little house awhile?" He raised his voice.

She stopped and, turning to him, took a deep breath and said, "You don't know me!"

"So what?"

"So, I'm a stranger to you!"

"So what? I ain't asking you to move in with me." The humor returned to his voice. "Just use the cottage!"

Vilma looked at the cottage a moment. "I don't have much money!"

"Don't need much!" he smiled.

"I can't pay you any rent." Her voice was low.

"So what? Ain't no rent! I dont owe nothin on it, so neither do you!" He smiled again.

"Welllll." Vilma took a few steps toward the cottage.

"Now. That's better!" He reached for her suitcase. She pulled back.

"Now, I'm not going to be no second-hand wife."

"So what?" he smiled gently.

"I mean it! And I am not cooking!"

"So what?"

"I'm not doing any kind of work!"

"So what?" He reached again for the suitcase.

"And I'm sleeping in the cottage and you are sleeping in that house . . . every night!" She pointed as she spoke, seriously.

"Alright!" he answered with patience.

"I am not going to make love with you, Jacob."

"So what? Vilma, I didn't ask you to." He took the suitcase and walked her back to the cottage.

And that day she got settled in. They passed each other, now and then, but didn't talk; he just smiled, she looked concerned, but happy . . . and she was.

Over one breakfast, which he cooked, he said, "You gonna get tired out here with nothing to do."

"Oh, no I'm not. I've been waiting all my life for nothing to do!"

"You just going to sleep?" he continued.

95

"No! There's plenty to do. Besides," she laughed, "So what?"

She decorated the cottage with flowers and leaves, planting wild flowers in bottles and jars and hanging them around the eaves of the little house. Rocks were made into designs around the yard with novel pieces of wood. Feathers were made into bouquets in odd little containers. She had improvised a bird bath and to her great delight, the birds used it. She visited the fat brown cows and petted their warm skins and shooed flies away from their eyes. She fed the chickens and had a favorite rooster that she felt was so dressed-up in his checkered-looking black and white suit with the sharp red hat, he walked like he owned the chickenyard. She called him Highstepper, and he began to answer her call. A cat from somewhere attached itself to her; it came every morning and she fed it, then they sat together each with their own thoughts till each evening the cat would go away to something somewhere of its own.

Happiness and peacefulness just grew out and bubbled all over the backyard and down the back road leading to the pond where she fished sometime and brought dinner home. Two months passed in this way and she forgot to leave, to follow the sunset. She had her own private sunset every evening, all evening. Why, even if she lay in bed, right there through her windows, through her trees, she watched it.

Then, one day, Jacob went to town and brought back a bottle of gin, a pack of beer and a box of candy, among other things.

The gin and soda water loaded with ice was good and they laughed as they drank and listened to some old records on the phonograph he brought out in the backyard. Then the gin was gone and the beer was good and cold as they laughed and she tried to show him some dances she had done down through the years. He laughed and laughed and looked and looked. When she said, "I think I'm getting high," he said, "So what?" and they laughed together. Then she was in the cottage, somehow, and he was trying to make love to her. She wanted him to stop, but didn't feel like fighting him . . . he had been good to her. No . . . she didn't love him in that way, but he had been good to her, two good months. Yes, she was free to fuck who she wanted to, but she wanted someone to give her love to, someone who made her star twinkle, as in "twinkle, twinkle, little star." He didn't make her star twinkle, but he did make it burn brighter, so she let him make love to her. So what?

Vilma had planned to pack and leave the next day, but she didn't. She just didn't. Besides, he didn't come near her at night. Things had gone back to normal. Maybe I can stay a little longer, she said, knowing even then she was going to have to go. But she didn't. The time passed and that night of lovemaking turned into old lovemaking and Vilma was comfortable again. Then the rain came with the thunder and the lightning and the wind. He knocked, but even as she answered, "What do you want?" she knew, and when she said, "We can't do this, I am not your wife or your woman!" he said, "So what? You are who I love!" as he made love to her. When they were through and he lay upon her, soaking in the warmth and her scent and his sweat, she rubbed his head and back tenderly and said to herself, "So what?"

The next day, she stayed in bed and watched the rain dry from the leaves and the ground. She also stayed in bed the next day and the next, just staring out of the window at the sunrise, the sunlight and the sunset through the trees. He finally came over to see if she was alright, when she said she was, he said, "Why don't you come on over to the house? Why don't you cook some food for a change? Let me see how you can cook." She didn't say anything, just looked out the window again, then he left. She rose and started packing her suitcase, then looked around the room she had called home for awhile. She saw things she wanted to take with her, but didn't want to be attached to anything! So she left it. The cat hadn't been around since the storm so she couldn't say good-bye to it. She started out of the yard meaning to come back and say, thank you and good-bye, when her car was ready to go. Jacob met her as she walked into the dirt drive and he snatched her bag from her hand and grabbed her blouse and pulled and jerked her back to the cottage. The buttons flew, the seams tore and she was screaming at him, but still he dragged her and threw her into the cottage and shoved her into the wall, then he went out and got the suitcase and threw it against the wall.

"You ain't leaving me! No one else is gonna leave me!" he said; he was crying, too.

"I've got to go, Jacob, I've got to go. You knew I was not here to stay forever!" she pleaded. She saw the fist coming and even then, she felt sorry for him. Where was his "So what?" when she needed it? Why had he run out of "So whats?" when she needed only one more? Then she lost consciousness. When she woke up again, he was sitting beside her bed, she was cleaned and dressed in her gown, her head bandaged and there was medicine, doctor's medicine, on the bedtable.

"Oh God, I'm sorry Vilma, I didn't mean to hurt you. I got the doctor. I been taking care of you. I love you. I'm sorry!"

Vilma said nothing, her lips were sore anyway. She just looked at him.

"Don't leave me, Vilma. I need you here with me. You ain't got nowhere to go, no way. You gonna stay here with me . . . please."

Vilma just looked at him. She tried to hate him, but was glad to find in her heart she couldn't. She felt sorry for him, that's all. She turned her head to the window and slept. He cared for her and the cat for almost two weeks, then she felt a lot better and moved around. Though she spoke very seldom, he talked all the time, trying to make her comfortable again.

The day she put her bag in the car, he only put his hands

in his coveralls and watched her. He saw the cat follow her and jump into the car and as he walked over to the car he heard her tell the cat, "I'm not telling you to come with me, come if you want to, but I won't own you! I'll feed you when I eat, that's all!" The cat sat still on the seat so Vilma got in and shut the door just as the cat began to move, perhaps to get out. He put his hand on her shoulder just as she began to stroke the cat.

"Don't go, Vilma," he said, but she started the car.

"Don't go, Vilma," he said. She looked in his face as the cat jumped out the window to its freedom. She smiled.

"I love you, Vilma."

"So what?" she said softly, and drove away to her freedom.

      *   *   *

This story also has two endings. That's one.

About a year or maybe six months later, Vilma turned around and started looking after the sunrise again. That made her come back toward that little cottage, you know? When she got there, the place looked a little run down, not much, but a little like someone maybe didn't care so much. So what? But he came out to the driveway, the dirt one, and just stood there looking at her. She smiled and the angels did sing. She leaned on her car.

"You got a woman living in there yet?" she pointed to his house.

"No." He shook his head "no," too.

She reached into the car and pulled her suitcase out.

"Where can I put my suitcase?" she held it in both arms.

"Anywhere!" with a glimmer of a smile.

"I'll start out in that little cottage of mine, I believe." She started walking slowly up the drive to the back.

He didn't say anything, just took the bag from her when she reached where he was and turned to walk beside her until they reached the cottage then he handed it to her, showing her he was not going to come in where he wasn't wanted, I guess. The cottage was all clean, everywhere!

"How come this house is all cleaned up? You expecting somebody?" She got kind of nervous.

"Expecting, and hoping, it was for you," he was serious again.

"You thought I'd come back?" She sat the suitcase down and turned to look at him.

"I prayed . . . you'd come back." You could see he had.

"So . . . that's who was bothering me every day!" She sat down on the bed with a heavy sigh, like she wasn't sure she had done the right thing. "I've changed my name, you know!" She smiled up at him. "It's Vilma Twinkle now."

"You got married?" You could feel his tension.

"No . . . just a little private joke of mine." She looked at him hard. He didn't crack a smile either. Finally she looked away.

"Well, I'm back." After all, she had to say something.

"And, I am tired, I've driven all day and all night!"

"Go to bed, get some rest, I'll get you something to eat," he was beginning to smile now.

"No, I brought something with me, it's in the car. You might want some." She lay back on the bed and when she looked up again, he was gone and the door was closed.

The next morning, he didn't wake her, just looked in on her . . . she hadn't locked the door. When she did wake up and look outside, the yard was clean again and she could smell food cooking and somehow things looked like they had the first time she had seen them. He was coming around the corner of the house with some tool, humming and smiling to himself.

"Hey!" she spoke to him. "What you doing?"

"Hey," he answered, smiling. "Just cleaning things up a bit."

She leaned against the doorjamb with one arm and put the other hand on her hip.

"Listen," she said, "No gin and no beer, I just want you to come here," and she stood there twinkling.

He dropped the tools but still stood there, smiling or grinning, whichever. "But you ain't my wife . . . yet," he said.

"So What?" she answered. And their laughter filled the yard and the cottage and the trees and their hearts.

Liberated

ONCE upon a time, not too long ago, but long enough, there lived Middy and James who had just celebrated their 40th wedding anniversary. They had married when James was 23 and Middy was 16 years of age. Middy was a smart young girl raised by solid parents til her daddy died and her mamma, being a strong woman, never missed a step. She kept right on working and taking care of her family with an extra job or two . . . tired, toiling but determined! I always say Middy took after her, except I knew Middy had big dreams for herself, I didn't know about her mama.

Yes, Middy dreamed she would go a long way in life but when she was 16, James came along, back from some war, even way back then. He had looked good, was strong and had deep healthy laughter. He had been raised by hard working parents and he was a solid hard-working man. He continued that way all his life. His mind had one direction . . . work, money and buying property. He was like a lotta people . . . a little work here, a little love there, these things was his excitement and his living and never changed. Several women were after him and that's probably what prompted Middy to get him first. She was one of them look-back-again girls, so she got him. She had always said she would be a virgin when she married, so when she lost her virginity, her mind and body followed. Some people said she was being foolish, but people can't tell you nothing for sure . . . Only time can! Anyway she tucked them dreams of hers back in third or fourth place.

Middy told the white woman she worked for after school that she was gonna get married and was leavin for good. The woman told her she would never be happy married to a poor black man, being used as a baby carrier and slave-worker woman. Ain't that somethin! Middy thought a moment about that and knew that she wasn't really liberated anyway, the only difference between James and the white woman was makin love! Other than the makin babies, everything else was the same. And making babies could be fun! Besides, she loved James. She left!

You know, life proved out that white woman never did find a man to marry her, least not around here. She had a child out of wedlock and left town!

Anyway, Middy married James and closed that part of her life that was her dreams. They had two children, a boy, now 38 years old, and a girl, now 35 years old. Several hundred times over the years she would be standin over a washtub, early in the morning as the sun comes up, stars still out, birds singing and flying through the air, flowers and weeds just opening up to drink the dew, and she would look way off into her own mind and them dreams just stole out, but she push em back. They come out again when she be hanging them clothes up, she push em back. She be standin over a hot stove, sweat running down her face, clothes sticking to her back and sides from the sweat of her body . . . them dreams come out, but she squeeze them back. Because she was lucky! James was a good man, working hard to take care of her and the children.

Work got lighter as the children grew up and moved away

to college, but it never did stop. Forty years of washing clothes, cooking, making love, grocery shopping, cleaning, ironing, making love, sewing, mending, making love, looking at TV, making sex and readin books. The first two years were exciting, the next four were good, the next 34 were O.K.! Thank God, it was O.K.

Finally, now, James was balding, treasured teeth left at the dentist. Both of them! Just changes! One thing at a time, one hair, one tooth. A piece of skin wrinkles here, another piece loosens there. A piece of brain sets, won't move again. Just things . . . don't you know?

James kept his wife, and home, satisfied but with no fringes. After being married 25 years he got an extra woman, Sally, who he also kept but gave none of the fringes to. Sally even paid a small rent. He insisted on that, saying his wife, Middy, would know if she, Sally, didn't pay. But he would give half of it back to her later and she, being a quiet and gentle type woman thought that was very nice and accepted it and was very nice back to him and remained faithful. She made him her own life. James always came to the house she rented from him to make love and he never took her anywhere, except fishin sometimes . . . his wife, you know. So she was very deeply involved in the church for her social life and the sewing circles, which three or four times a year went to the County Fairs. James really had a nice, even life and it suited him fine, leaving him time to work on his houses and use his truck to haul things to the junk yard for the white folks. He got a lot of clothes and furniture and stuff for his two women that way. He didn't really need or want another woman besides Middy, but there was a long-lived rumor still going round that a man had to have an extra woman on the side or he wasn't a man! So he had one . . . cause he sure was the man . . . in both houses . . . he said!

Now Middy was a small but energetic woman who did her work but, with the children being grown and gone, her life had been given over to readin books and magazines and looking at TV. She could care less about a sewing circle. She watched all the civil rights action and had wished she wasn't too old for it. And now, the last few years, television was full of liberated women and was about men and women being equal and all! In the talk shows she would shake her fist and scream and yell and argue with the TV and James would get less, whatever. She had already told him she wasn't gettin up cooking breakfast anymore, only dinner and several other little changes which didn't really bother James. He just attributed these things to "womenfolk" and went on over to Sally's for breakfast or whatever. Middy knew about Sally and at first, years ago, she was mad and scared but held her own council and soon after she had thought about it enough, she knew she wasn't going nowhere, she had a home for life. Besides, several times, she got looks at Sally who was a fairly nice-looking, clean woman, not a flaming Jezebel, so she decided to be quiet and accept the help. Let it be. Middy never thought of another man for herself, hell, she had one! He took better care of her than some of the women she knew. Besides, one little wiggling thing couldn't be too different from another little wiggling thing up there . . . so what for? Middy had never known another man to make love to, so she could make no comparisons. She would rather watch TV, read or work on her list. Middy kept a list of all the things she would do if she had money and was free. It was a long list but a few of the items were: a fur coat, learn to drive, get a car, a diamond ring, a diamond watch, silk underwear, go to Europe or India, a face lift, a real hairdresser and last, but not least, clothes made just for her or bought off the rack just for her! At that time all her clothes, even the dress-up ones, were second hand from James' truck. Because James complained all the time of being broke she had quit bothering him, and after she checked to see if Sally was ever wearing anything new, and she wasn't ever, she just tried to look the best she could in what she had and did her own hair and shopped at the Five and Dime for her perfumes and creams. She liked to bathe and cream her body all over, put her perfume on over her patched nightgowns and sip a little cheap wine out of the chipped crystal glass (from the truck) before she went to sleep. Champagne was on her list. That TV really was her window to the world. She was 56 and holding on to her living for dear life. James often told her, after some declaration or argument of hers, that she was watching too much TV but she would laugh and say she "never would see too much TV! TV was a liberator!" Well, that's how the last 10 years or so passed. Life goes on, you know, and on and on and on for some.

One day the television broke at the same time the library books were all read. The repair man came and said it was gone for good, they needed a new one. James said "No, they couldn't afford it" "Maybe next month, or so." He really should have run down then and got another one but, instead, he laughed to himself as he said "Not right now, can't afford it!" Well Middy turned herself to doing things around the house that you really never feel like doing. Cleaning out drawers and closets. Not just hers, but James' also. Now happy accidents are almost only somethin you read about, but sometimes they really do happen! That's what happened to Middy! As she was throwing James' clothes across the bed to clean his closet a bank book fell on the floor. She picked it up with no special interest because she knew they had a little money in the bank. James often showed the book to her. But when she took it from its case and opened it, it was not the same book . . . this one was still in both their names, but it had $38,978 listed as balance. Middy thought at first there was some mistake or a joke book, but her hands just kept moving with a life all their own and she went through those clothes and found the other book he had always shared with her. It had $2000 as balance. She put all the clothes back, struck too dumb to even think about cleaning anything. She was in a daze. She replaced both books in his clothes and went to the kitchen and drank all the rest of her little cheap wine and went to bed, drunk!

It was at least two weeks or a month before Middy had formed her plans. During that time, James would catch her looking at him in wonder (she hadn't told him she knew) and ask "Whats wrong with you?" and she would answer "Nothing wrong with me!" She was thinking now about all them little pieces of property he had rented out and how long he had been doing carpentry work and hauling things in his truck . . . 40 years! More than a thousand dollars a year he had saved! And still sent the kids to college and all! But she also thought of all he had made her do without, so he could save money! It was good . . . but not so good when she thought she had passed the age to enjoy some things that she would never be of an age to enjoy again! Just passed! Gone! Somehow, she knew, if this bank book with $38,000 was in her name also, all the property was too, cause if he was going to hold anything back to call his own, it would have been the money! After a few calls, anonymous, to the bank to find out how accounts worked and if she could withdraw any money, she learned about the "and/or" business and checking the bankbook it said "or", somebody's mistake, the clerk's, not James'. Now when she pulled her list out, and she did that often now, she smiled all through her little body, head to toes. The next fishing trip James planned, he would be gone all day and all night. She was ready. She went to the bank with the book and started to withdraw $18,000 but changed to $20,000 because he would have the other account of $2000. She wanted cash! The bank said "What a large amount for cash!" Middy calmly replied James sent her for cash because he was buying another piece of property and the seller wanted CASH. They told her to come back in an hour and she did. Then she took a bus to another small town and got a safe deposit box and put $18,000 in it and came home, but not before she signed up for driving lessons and bought herself a large diamond ring and watch, a bottle of champagne and a NEW satin nightgown! All the rest of that day she glittered and sipped and ate a Filet Mignon steak with all the trimmings and read a stack of the latest NEW fashion magazines. Bought and paid for by herself! Hadn't no rich white woman read or used them first. Everything was put away in the morning.

When James returned, laughing under his brain at how smart he was and how he fooled Middy and had enjoyed his little trip with Sally, they sat over cups of coffee, smiling at each other!

Middy wasn't worried about James finding out . . . she wasn't scared of him and it was rightfully half hers! But oddly enough, the bank didn't say a word to James. Thought he would know about his own money, I guess. She did think he would take the ring and watch if he knew, so she did not wear them. She learned how to drive while he was busy at work, then went to her safe deposit box and took half the cost of a new car out and put the other half on credit . . . after all half was his. She parked it in a safe place and went home.

It was now time to go see a little of the world. She felt some pity for Sally and wanted to go talk to her but decided to leave well enough alone and didn't. She announced she was going to visit the daughter who taught school over in Atlanta. James smiled and said "that is nice," so after he left for work or wherever, she got in her car and drove to Atlanta, went shopping at the best stores, bought a suitcase and packed it in the store! The salesgirls laughed at her behind their hands but she didn't even see them cause she was fulfilling HER dreams, not theirs! She drove on to her daughter's, whose mouth opened in surprise when her mother drove up and announced she had come to see some City Life, some of the World! The daughter was just a country girl living in the city so the places she took her mother were ordinary places. A restaurant here, a nightclub or two there, very ordinary places. Middy asked her daughter, "This what an education and a good job got you? This kind of life? What's exciting in your life?" But campus parties and drinking and makin love were what her daughter had been doing since her divorce and she really did not know what her mother was talkin about, so her mother left her, sayin "Better save your money so you can learn to do somethin someday fore you get too old! It comes a time when it's too late for dreams . . . makin em or makin them come true!" Daughter laughed and said "I don't have to worry mama, daddy told me I'll be well taken care of when he die!" Middy drove off, scarf flying in the wind, saying "He got to take care me first!" Middy stopped to get "just one more little thing" before leaving that shopping heaven and right next door was a travel agency. She went in and browsed a minute or two then pulled a page torn from her fashion magazines from her purse . . . a trip to Europe. Mostly Paris, France, but including Greece and Switzerland! She left the agency saying the "money will be forthcoming!" She drove home.

James was sitting on the porch . . . looking as if he had been dragged across fifty miles of hard road. He had even been cryin. The first thing he said was "Middy, where my money?" "What money?" Middy asked, deciding to leave her bag in the car. "Where you get that car? Whose car is that?" She started to answer "Ours" but changed to "Mine! you like it?" "No I don't! Where is my money? That what you doin with it? Spending it on every foolish thing? Spending it?" Tears in his voice.

Middy took a deep breath and resigned herself to go through whatever was to come with as little trouble as possible.

"That's what money is for James, to spend if you need to and to save if you don't need it."

James was almost crying again. "I spose you NEEEEEDED that car?"

109

"You got a car and a truck, James."

"I work . . I need them . . . sides theys yours too!"

"I couldn't even drive, James. Wasn't no car mine!"

"Why didn't you tell me what you wanted?"

"Been tellin you 40 years, James."

"Well . . . gimmie the rest of the money and keep the car and all the rest them things you bought up there in Atlanta with our daughter! But gimmie the rest! I'll see can I put things back together!" He held out his hand.

"What is that money for, James?" Middy looked up at James.

"Our children, Middy, yours and mine!" Hand still held out.

"We paid for their education, James. They can get their own!" She was still standing at the bottom of the porch steps. Suitcases still in the car, too heavy for her to carry and she didn't want to ask James to carry them!

James sighed and wiped his brow. He didn't look like the proud owner of two women anymore.

"Gimmie that money back Middy! I worked for that money Middy! Give it else I'm a hafta keep myself from half killin you! I mean it!" His nose was runnin now and he didn't care.

Middy sighed and wiped her brow under the pretty scarf blowing in the breeze. "Can't James! Just can't. Done worked for that money right long side of you. Its mine too! And . . . if you almost kill me . . . I'll go to court and take half these houses and that will kill you" She didn't shout tho, she talked soft, but firm. James snarled through snot and tears, but he did not move to half kill Middy.

Middy came up a step. "James," she said softly, "You ain't never gone nowhere in 40 years you wasn't wearin something I washed, ironed, sewed or hung up or folded. Not in 40 years without somethin I hadn't cooked, cleaned, stirred and shopped, in your body. I made the bed you sleep in every night for 40 years!" Her voice almost lost control and shouted, but she caught it. "I am your wife . . . was your wife before them kids was your kids. I'm the one you spose to work for and with now. We did it for them already! I'm suppose to be more than a maid or a cook or a flat back in your bed! We work for each other!" She lost control, the voice went on up. "The kids have 40 or 50 years more to get what we got! We don't! I'm going to live a little before I get on away from this earth! You can come if you want to, but if you don't I'm goin anyway! Got to go! Been dreamin about things all my life! If you goin to make any more dreams come true, James, they sposed to be your own and your woman's!"

James' hand was still out but his head was bowed down to his knees and he was rockin back and forth and wasn't in no rockin chair! Middy kept on coming, "I love my children . . . but to hell with them kids! They still gonna have plenty when I die! And the most important thing they will have is BREATH! To fill their own dreams and plans!"

James, a truly responsible man, bowed his head lower and cried. He wanted to hit her so hard her head would soar and fly like a bird . . . but he didn't want to divide his property . . . so he cried. Middy went on in the house and called the travel agency.

In a few weeks, after many hours of silence with James dragging around, losing weight and sometimes snapping at her, punishing her by eating dinner out (over at Sally's, who thought he was falling more in love with her and out of love with Middy), Middy drove her car to Atlanta, bought a fur coat, put the car in storage and boarded a plane bound for Europe. She sat in the seat, her list and plenty money in her purse which she patted unconsciously . . . she cried. Not from pity for James, not from fear . . . but for the joy in her heart at being able to live a few of her dreams. She thanked James in her heart for being the kind of man he was . . . a saving man. As the plane moved out on the runway and gathered speed to lift itself to the skies, Middy looked through the bright window, smiled through her tears . . . and flew away.

Switzerland first, for a rejuvenation program. Mud packed, mud bathed, massaged, exercised, coifed, manicured, relaxed, handled gently but body coaxed somehow into looking like she had always wanted to look. Waking to a soft knock on her door, someone bringing fresh juice and fruits and breads ten minutes old, eating beside a window out of which mountains stretched to forever, sparkling white with snow. Tall green trees everywhere dripping icicles while inside her room the fireplace crackled with flames of warmth. Middy snuggled down into her satin covered bed and thought to herself "I never even dreamed of this" and slept. Oh My, she looked good when she left there two weeks later. On to Paris to a splendid hotel. She decided not to spend money on clothes made custom for her, she'd rather travel! There were beautiful clothes everywhere anyway!

The gentlemen in Paris, wealthy and middle class, looked interestedly at the little, healthy, brighteyed, brownskinned well-dressed woman and sent flowers to her room and champagne to her table. She glowed and gleamed and spoke haltingly in French and English, sipped champagne held in the hand of the sparkling diamond ring and watch, to which diamond earrings had been added and one stone at her throat. They smiled in anticipation beneath their mustaches, but she allowed no one in her room after light dancing in the night clubs was over. She kissed once or twice, her few false teeth firmly glued in place. Ohhh and the French perfume she wore! Her nose was as happy as the rest of her.

The one man she noticed most, sent the most flowers, candy and champagne, but beyond a nod and smile, never approached her. She began to look for him in the lobby or dining room. One morning near the end of her stay (she had cancelled out Greece but still the time was coming to leave Paris) she came down for breakfast and passing him with a smile where he sat with his roll and coffee, she stopped and said "Bon Jour!" He answered, "Good Morning." He was French, however. Being the kind of black woman I know, she went directly to the point. "Why are you so generous to me with flowers and candy and champagne, yet you never say anything to me?"

He replied, standing and indicating the seat opposite him, "Will you join me for your breakfast?"

"Yes," she said, laughing softly, "I will, thank you."

She sat and asked again, "Why?"

He answered with a question, "Why?"

"Why do you send so many pleasant thoughts and never speak to me?"

He said, "I was waiting."

She said, "Waiting? For what?"

He smiled, "For you to come to me."

She smiled, "And so I did. Too aggressive!"

He smiled, "Too slow! But you are here."

She said, "Well . . . now . . . what were you waiting for?"

He said, "To spend my day with you."

She laughed lightly, pleased and smiling, then she raised the crystal glass of sparkling water to him, with the ice tinkling as she pressed it to her lips.

They spent the day at the Louvre and the sidewalk cafes between the sights he showed to her. Paris! It was a beautiful city. The evening was spent over dinner and wine with many glasses of champagne later at the club he took her to hear soft singing entertainment. The few remaining days were spent in much the same way. All pleasant. The last day before she was to leave, he stayed the night. I cannot describe it to you for I am not a poet. It was different and it was good. Perhaps because of the luxury hotel, the beautiful days spent doing beautiful things with delightful meals in lovely clothes, perhaps the expensive champagne. She had not even known this lovemaking was on her list of dreams, but she thrilled to all his touches and the woman in her who was neither young nor old, was passionate, thrilled and satisfied beyond even her knowledge of her dreams. She left the next day. For home? Where was home? On arriving in Atlanta much later, she cried again . . . for a different reason.

When she got home Sally was there with James. He said, "This ain't your home no more. You done left it, so go on away somewhere again, you got your money!" She answered, "Going away six weeks don't pay for forty years! Go on to your house Sally, this one is mine!" James grunted but took Sally home. He came back to argue all night with Middy and even try to make love. She let him, but she stayed aware of how he felt to her. It was good . . . and comfortable, but there was no feeling except one of familiarity and that was not enough anymore, somehow.

Her thoughts in the next two or three months were so tangled. She drove a lot, going nowhere, walked a lot, going nowhere. Laid awake a lot, saying to herself, "Now listen here, enough is enough!" Herself answered back, "What's enough?"

One day she went back to the bank and got out enough money from James' account and went to the lawyers and paid $3000 for the house Sally lived in and deeded it to Sally. Then she got a bottle of champagne, went to Sally's house to tell her and give her a copy of the deed.

She told Sally, "You better do something for yourself before it's too late!"

Sally said, "But I'm going on 50 years old!"

Middy answered, "That's what I mean . . . you still got time . . don't waste it! And another thing, I may still want my husband! Now you got your own house, so don't ever move in mine again!"

Sally said, "I sure won't! I rather have my own anyway!"

Middy said, "That's smart. Stay that way!" They finished the champagne and Middy left, leaving Sally high as a kite with a smile on her face.

Middy then went to a piece of their property she particularly liked and told the people they had 30 days to move, to keep their last month's rent and find a new place. When they had moved, she went in and had it all redone. New paint, new wallpaper, new stove, just new everything! All out of her own money.

James was fightin mad and arguing and screaming all the time. Couldn't hardly work, but did. Had his own bank account now, all by himself. But signed the proper deeds for the little house Middy wanted for her own in exchange for her letting all his other future property alone til he died. However all the property and its income was still half hers. She told him, "Take it and do what you want with it when you buy property, just see that I always have some money." She still takes care of all his home needs . . . when she is home.

She commenced to take them trips every six months or so. She go to Africa and Greece and France and everywhere. She took up that sculpture and some painting classes. Sometimes she stay for two months or so. Lately she been stayin six months. House just full of things she bring back to sell. Say she may stay forever one day. Brings me back some material, beautiful, that some woman in Africa makes, cause I love to sew and knit.

I'm her friend, thats why I know all about it and two years ago, when I was forty-seven years old, I got out and got me a job cause my husband never did save no money! He just always in the street playin after he put in his eight hours! Ain't spent no time with me in years and years. The TV says he takes me for granted . . . say he neglects me! So I been saving my money, ain't spent a dime on nothin but what I really, really, really need! It all goes in the bank! Made my reservation for that place in Switzerland for the rejuvenation, then I'm going on to Africa. Middy has made me a appointment with that lady who makes the homemade material and I'm going to learn it and maybe start a little

115

business of my own. Leavin two days from now! My list ain't long as Middy's, but my money ain't neither and I'ma have to come back and work again, but I don't care! I'm going where none of the people in my family ever been! I'm going to fly! My mama ain't never had a chance to do that either, now she is dead and never will have a chance! That map I learned in school, when I could go, gonna mean somethin to me after all these years.

You may not think so, but liberated is somethin!

Middy is liberated!

I can't hardly wait! I'm gettin liberated too!

A Jewel for a Friend

I HAVE my son bring me down here to this homegrown graveyard two or three times a week so I can clean it and sweep it and sit here among my friends in my rocking chair under this Sycamore tree, where I will be buried one day, soon now, I hope. I'm 90 years old and I am tired . . . and I miss all my friends too. I come back to visit them because ain't nobody left in town but a few old doddering fools I didn't bother with when I was younger so why go bothern now just cause we all hangin on? Its peaceful here. The wind is soft, the sun is gentle even in the deep summer. Maybe its the cold that comes from under the ground that keeps it cool. I don't know. I only know that I like to rest here in my final restin place and know how its gonna be a thousand years after I am put here under that stone I have bought and paid for long ago . . . long ago.

After I eat my lunch and rest a bit, I gets down to my real work here in this graveyard! I pack a hammer and chisel in my bags and when I's alone, I take them and go over to Tommy Jones' beautiful tombstone his fancy daughter bought for him and chip, grind and break away little pieces of it! Been doin it for eleven years now and its most half gone. I ain't gonna die til its all gone! Then I be at peace! I ain't got to tell a wise one that I hate Tommy Jones, you must know that yourself now!. .If I am killin his tombstone! I hate him. See, his wife, my friend, Pearl, used to lay next to him, but I had her moved, kinda secret like, least without tellin anyone. I hired two mens to dig her coffin up and move her over here next to where I'm going to be and they didn't know nobody and ain't told nobody. It don't matter none noway cause who gon pay somebody to dig her up again? And put her back? Who cares bout her? . . . and where she lay for eternity? Nobody! But me . . . I do.

See, we growed up together. I am Ruby and she is Pearl and we was jewels. We use to always say that. We use to act out how these jewels would act. I was always strong, deep red and solid deep. She was brown but she was all lightness and frail and innocent, smooth and weak and later on I realized, made out of pain.

I grew up in a big sprawling family and my sons take after them, while Pearl growed up in a little puny one. Her mama kissed her daddy's ass til he kicked her's on way from here! That's her grave way over there . . . Way, way over there in the corner. That's his with that cement marker, from when he died two years later from six bullets in his face by another woman what didn't take that kickin stuff! Well, they say what goes around . . . But "they" says all kinda things . . . can't be sure bout nothin "they" says. Just watch your Bible . . . that's the best thing I ever seen and I'm 90! Now!

Anyway, Pearl and me grew up round here, went to school and all. A two room school with a hall down the middle. Pearl nice and everybody should of liked her, but they didn't. Them girls was always pickin on her, til I get in it. See, I was not so nice and everybody did like me! Just loved me sometime! I pertected her. I wouldn't let nobody hurt her! Some of em got mad at me, but what could they do? I rather fight than eat! Use to eat a'plenty too! I was a big strong, long-armed and long-legged girl. Big head, short hair. I loved my eyes tho! Oh, they was pretty. They still strong! And I had pretty hands, even with all that field work, they still was pretty! My great grandchildren takes care of em for me now . . . rubs em and all. So I can get out here two or three times a week and hammer Tommy Jones' gravestone. Its almost half gone now . . . so am I.

When we got to marryin time . . . everybody got to that, some in love and some just tryin to get away from a home what was full of house work and field work and baby sister and brother work. I don't know how we was all too dumb to know, even when we got married and in a place of our own, it was all headin down to the same road we thought we was gettin away from! Well, I went after Gee Cee! He was the biggest boy out there and suited me just fine! I use to run that man with rocks and sticks and beat him up even. He wouldn't hurt me, you know, just play. But I finally got him to thinkin he loved me and one night, over there by the creek behind the church, way behind the church, I gave him somethin he musta not forgot . . . and we was soon gettin married. I didn't forget it . . . I named it George, Jr. That was my first son.

In the meantime the boys all seem to like Pearl and she grinned at all of em! She seem to be kinda extra stuck on that skinny rail, Tommy Jones, with the bare spot on the side of his head! He liked everybody! A girl couldn't pass by him without his hand on em, quick and fast and gone. I didn't like him! Too shifty for me . . . a liar! I can't stand a liar! His family had a little money and he always looked nice but he still wasn't nothin but a nice lookin liar what was shifty! Still and all, when I had done pushed Pearl around a few times tryin to make her not like him, he began to press on her and every way she turned, he was there! He just wouldn't let up when he saw I didn't like him for her! He gave her little trinkets and little cakes, flowers, home picked. Finally she let him in her deepest life and soon she was pregnant and then he got mad cause he had to marry her! I fought against that and when he found out it made him grin all the way through the little ceremony. I was her best lady or whatever you call it, cause I was her best friend.

Then everything was over and we was all married and havin children and life got a roll on and we had to roll with it and that took all our energies to survive and soon we was back in the same picture we had run away from cept the faces had changed. Stead of mama's faces, they was ours. And daddy's was the men we had married. Lots of times the stove and sink was the same and the plow was the same. In time, the mules changed.

Well, in time, everything happened. I had three sons and two daughters, big ones! Liked to kill me even gettin here! Pearl had one son and one daughter. Son was just like his daddy and daughter was frail and sickly. I think love makes you healthy and I think that child was sickly cause wasn't much love in that house of Pearl's, not much laughter. Tommy Jones, after the second child, never made love to Pearl again regular, maybe a year or two or three apart. She stayed faithful, but hell, faithful to what? He had done inherited some money and was burnin these roads up! He'd be a hundred miles away for a week or two, whole lotta times. Pearl worked, takin them children with her when I could'n keep em. But I had to rest sometimes, hell! I had five of my own and I had done told her bout that Tommy Jones anyway! But I still looked out for her and fed em when she couldn't. Yet and still, when he came home he just fall in the bed and sleep and sleep til time to get up and bathe and dress in the clothes he bought hisself and leave them again! If she cry and complain he just laugh and leave. I guess that's what you call leavin them laughin or somethin!

One day he slapped her and when he saw she wasn't gonna do nothin but just cry and take it, that came to be a regular thing! For years, I mean years, I never went over her house to take food when she didn't have some beatin up marks on her! I mean it! That's when she started comin over to the cemetery to clean it up and find her place. She also began savin a nickle here and a dime there to pay for her gravestone. That's what she dreamed about! Can you imagine that?!! A young, sposed to be healthy woman daydreamin bout dyin!!? Well, she did! And carried that money faithfully to the white man sells them things and paid on a neat little ruby colored stone, what he was puttin her name on, just leavin the dates out! Now!

My sons was gettin married, havin babies, strong like they mama and papa, when her son got killed, trying to be like his daddy! He had done screwed the wrong man's daughter! They put what was left of him in that grave over there, behind that bush of roses Pearl planted years ago to remember him by. Well, what can I say? I'm a mother, she was a mother, you love them no matter what! The daughter had strengthened up and was goin on to school somewhere with the help of her father's people. And you know, she didn't give her mother no concern, no respect? Treated her like the house dog in a manger. I just don't blieve you can have any luck like that! It takes time, sometime, to get the payback, but time is always rollin on and one day, it will roll over you! Anyway even when the daughter had made it up to a young lady and was schoolin with the sons and daughters of black business people, she almost forgot her daddy too! She was gonna marry a man with SOMETHIN and she didn't want them at the weddin! Now! And tole em! Her daddy went anyway, so she dressed him cause he was broke now, and after the weddin, got his drunk ass out of town quick as lightnin cross the sky and he came home and taunted Pearl that her own daughter didn't love her! Now!

Well, time went on, I had troubles with such a big family, grandchildren comin and all. Love, love, love everywhere, cause I didn't low nothin else! Pretty faces, pretty smiles, round, fat stomachs, and pigtails flying everywhere and pretty nappy-headed boys growin up to be president someday, even if they never were .. they was my presidents and congressmen! I could chew em up and swollow em sometimes, even today, grown as they are! We could take care of our problems, they was just livin problems ... everyday kinds.

Pearl just seem to get quiet way back in her mind and heart. She went on, but she was workin harder to pay for that tombstone. The name was complete, only the last date was open and finally it was paid for. With blood, sweat and tears for true . . . seem like that's too much to pay for dyin!

One night I had bathed and smelled myself up for that old hard head of mine, Gee Cee, when a neighbor of Pearl's came runnin over screamin that Tommy Jones was really beatin up on Pearl. I threw my clothes on fast as I could and ran all the way and I was comin into some age then, runnin was not what I planned to do much of! When I got there, he had done seen me comin and he was gone, long gone, on them long, narrow, quick to run to mischief feet of his! I had got there in time to keep him from accidently killin her, but she was pretty well beat! He had wanted her rent and food money, she said, but she would not give it to him, so he beat her. She cried and held on to me, she was so frail, so little, but she was still pretty to me, little grey hairs and all. She thanked me as I washed her and changed the bed and combed her hair and fed her some warm soup and milk. She cried a little as she was tellin me all she ever wanted was a little love like I had. I cried too and told her that's all anybody wants.

When I was through fixin her and she was restin nice and easy, I sat by the bed and pulled the covers up and she said, "Hold my hand, I'm so cold." Well I grabbed her hand and held, then I rubbed her arms tryin to keep her warm and alive. Then, I don't know, life just kept rollin and I began to rub her whole little beautiful sore body ... all over ... and when I got to them bruised places I kissed them and licked them too and placed my body beside her body in her bed and the love for her just flowed and flowed. One minute I loved her like a child, the next like a mother, then she was the mother, then I was the child, then as a woman friend, then as a man. Ohhhhh, I loved her. I didn't know exactly what to do but my body did it for me and I did everything I could to make her feel loved and make her feel like Gee Cee makes me feel, so I did everything I could that he had ever done to me to make me feel good, but I forgot Gee Cee . . . and I cried. Not sad crying, happy cryin, and my tears and my love were all over her and she was holding me. She was holding me . . . so close, so close. Then we slept and when I wakened up, I went home . . . and I felt good, not bad. I know you don't need nothin "forever", just so you get close to love sometime.

Well Pearl got better. When we saw each other, we weren't embarrassed or shamed. She hit me on my shoulder and I thumped her on her head as we had done all our lives anyway. We never did it again, we didn't have to!

Pearl wasn't made, I guess, for the kind of life she had somehow chosen, so a few years later she died and Tommy Jones picked her plot, right over there where she used to be, and put her there and the tombstone man put that old-brand-new ruby colored gravestone on her grave. The preacher said a few words cause there wasn't much to pay him with and we all went home to our own lifes, of course.

Soon, I commence to comin over here and sweepin and cleanin up and plantin plants around and this ole Sycamore tree, Pearl had planted at her house, was moved over here before Tommy Jones got put out for not payin rent. I planted it right here over where Gee Cee, me and Pearl gonna be. I likes shade. Anyway I was out here so much that's how I was able to notice the day Pearl's tombstone disappeared. Well, I like to died! I knew what that tombstone had gone through to get there! Right away I had my sons get out and find out what had happened and they found out that Tommy Jones was livin mighty hard and was mighty broke and had stole that tombstone and took it way off and sold it for a few dollars! You can chisel the name off, you know? But I can't understand what anyone would want a used tombstone for! I mean, for God's sake, get your own!! At least die first-class even if you couldn't live that way! Well, we couldn't find how to get it back so that's when I started payin on another one for her, and yes, for me and Gee Cee too. They's paid for now.

In the meantime, liquor and hard livin and a knife put Tommy Jones to rest, and imagine this, that daughter of theirs came down here and bought ONE gravestone for her DADDY!!! To hold up her name I guess, but that's all she did, then she left! Ain't been back!

Well, life goes on, don't it! Whew!

Now I come here over the years and chip away and chisel and hammer away cause he don't deserve no stone since he stole Pearl's. He never give her nothin but them two babies what was just like him and then he stole the last most important thing she wanted! So me, I'm gonna see that he don't have one either! When it's through, I'm gonna be through, then the gravestone man can bring them two stones over here, they bought and paid for! And he can place them here beside each other, for the rest of thousands of years. I'm in the middle, between Gee Cee and Pearl, like I'm sposed to be. They don't say much, but Ruby and the dates and Pearl's on hers, and the dates. Then my husband's name and the children on mine and her children's on hers. And that's all. I mean, how much can a gravestone say anyway?

AFTERWORD

After Ruby died at 91 years of age, Gee Cee was still living at 90 years of age and he had a marker laid across the two graves saying, "Friends, all the way to the End." It's still there.

About the Author

J. California Cooper is the author of three collections of stories—
Some Soul to Keep, *Homemade Love* (a recipient of the 1989 American
Book Award), and *The Matter Is Life*—as well as a novel, *Family*, and
seventeen plays, many of which have been produced and per-
formed on the stage, public television, radio, and college cam-
puses. Her plays have also been anthologized, and in 1978 she was
named Black Playwright of the Year for *Strangers*, which was per-
formed at the San Francisco Palace of Fine Arts. Among her
numerous awards are the James Baldwin Writing Award (1988) and
the Literary Lion Award from the American Library Association
(1988). Ms. Cooper lives in a small town in Texas, and is the mother
of a daughter, Paris Williams.